THE MESSAGE
By Lance Richardson

Copyright © 2000   Lance M. Richardson

ALL RIGHTS RESERVED.
No part of this book may be reproduced in any form or by any means
without permission in writing from the publisher,
American Family Publishing, Idaho Falls, Idaho 83401
USA 1-888-583-9609 • (208) 522-2975

ISBN: 1-889025-04-6 (pb)
First Printing, December 2000

Printed in the United States of America.

THIS BOOK
IS DEDICATED TO

Dr. Kenneth Krell & staff,
Dr. Douglas Whattmore & staff,
Dr. Peter Cannon & staff,
Dr. Boyd Hammond,
Dr. Michael Denyer,
and to the team of other doctors,
Eastern Idaho Regional Medical Center (EIRMC)
ICU nursing staff of EIRMC,
3rd & 5th floor nursing staffs of EIRMC,
Teton Home Health & Pharmacy,
Eastgate Drug Store,
therapists, medical assistants,
pharmacists, and technicians
who brought me back
from the brink of death,
saved my life, and helped me recover.

THANK YOU

FOR YOUR EXPERT SKILL AND CARE,
AND FOR GIVING COMPASSION AND ASSISTANCE
TO ME AND MY FAMILY IN OUR TIME OF GREAT NEED.

Acknowledgments

My sincere thanks for the untold hours spent
and support given to this project by so many.
Most sincere thanks to:

Dr. Doug and Kris Robison,
Bruce and Janiel Miller,
Ron and Bonnie McMillan,
Laurie Snyder,
Krista Groll,
Profile Media,
Mark and Teresa,
Kristi Hall,
Todd,
Pam,
My wife and children,
and
my Mother and Father

CHAPTER		PAGE

1 It Was Christmas Day 7

2 A Time for Joy 17

3 The Accident 47

4 Happy New Year? 35

5 Begging for Breath 47

6 A Most Glorious Abode 51

7 Waiting and Wondering 59

8 Learning By the Spirit 63

9 Music and Temples 71

10 While I Was Sleeping 77

11 Principles of a Zion Society 85

12 Soon, I'll Be Back 95

13 It's Really All True, Isn't It 101

14 Liberty 105

15 The Blessing 111

16 The Message 115

17 Return to Mortality 121

18 There is an Answer 139

PREFACE

I am living on borrowed time.

To those who know me well, this statement is meaningful. For those who do not know my story, let me explain. I was allowed the rare opportunity of dying, then living again. I have been given the chance to live again in order that I may give my account and to finish some assignments I have been given.

I have never struggled so much over the writing or telling of something as I have this, for it is intensely personal. To tell this story I must open some of the most private chambers of my soul. I do not share this lightly.

There are those parts which are sacred and must remain locked within me. These would be most inappropriate to share. Yet, there were a number of things to which I was commanded to add my witness and detail publicly. To that commission I must remain true.

Regardless how many times I have started and stopped in the writing of this story, the promise I made to declare these things has driven me onward. I feel as if I were walking a tightrope in my attempt to remain faithful to my assignment, yet safeguard that which would be inappropriate to tell.

I have no desire to rally a following, for I am still the same weak and stumbling human that I was before; continually seeking to raise my life to the level that God desires, but ever recognizing my weaknesses and intense need for God's mercy and support.

I am completely incapable of answering a multitude of questions that I have been asked concerning the world hereafter and the reasons for so much of what occurs in our lives. Though I was granted a most incredible experience, my understanding and insight is yet so limited. The majority of these questions I must truthfully answer, "I do not know."

Yet, through all of this I have greatly added to my understanding and expanded my faith into an actual knowledge of some great and important truths. Yes, of a truth, my belief has become knowledge concerning certain things. And these have served to help me focus more fully upon undeniable things that really matter most. Indeed, this was one of the great truths I was given to learn; that there is so much in this world that we consider significant and worthy of our time and resources, which in reality means nothing. Ultimately, it is our families, our relationships, and how we are able to serve others that matter in the hereafter. It is not who we are, but how we live that matters eternally. It is not who we know, but how we love that counts in the world to come.

The Message which was shared with me is not prophetic; rather it is insightful and a strong reminder of truths which have been shared with us over the ages.

And so I now proceed with my attempt to fulfill my assignment and add my witness to some very important truths. I know that I must not fail, for I was given a chance to live again that I might do these things. I also know that I stand so desperately inadequate for the job. Yet, I must remain confident that the Lord knew this, too, when he allowed my return. To His commission, I must be true.

CHAPTER ONE

It Was Christmas Day

The snow was falling lightly to the ground when I first awakened. I peered through the corner of the curtains over our bedroom window and looked to the east. There would be no sunrise on this frozen white morning. The clouds blanketed the horizon with a dark grayish haze. I peered at my watch; it was nearly 5:30 on the morning of December 25th, Christmas Day, 1998. The thought brought a flood of memories to my mind of Christmas morns throughout my life.

I had always loved Christmas, and as a child had counted the days on the calendar for two months before the big day. But in recent years, I had missed some of the Christmases with my family. I had spent these holidays in the hospital trying to get control of a serious disease with which I continue to fight. Eighteen years previous I had contracted Crohn's Disease while living in Finland. It is not indigenous to that country. It is more prevalent in the United States. I was just unlucky enough to be part of a small group that developed the disease shortly after eating some raw salmon from the town, open-air market. Each of us remembered feeling severe pain, cramping, and diarrhea soon after eating the meat. I became extremely ill for a few months. Finally, I returned to the United States to get treatment. My father and I flew to the Mayo Clinic in Rochester, Minnesota, to see doctors who were considered to be the top specialists in the world with such problems. It was discovered that a group of people in Tampere, Finland, where I had been living, had picked up a parasite at the very same time as I had, which brought on the disease. By the time the doctors diagnosed the problem, however, the parasite was dead and gone. But the disease was clearly present.

This painful illness varies in its intensity from case to case. But, as one of my doctors at the Mayo Clinic told my father and me, my case was one of the most virulent he had ever seen. Though it can be severely painful, it usually does not cause death. "However," the Mayo Clinic doctor cautioned, "you may very well wish it did cause death, as painful as your case most likely will be." He had been correct in predicting the severity of my situation.

Over that eighteen year span I had endured approximately thirty major and minor surgeries for my disorder and its side effects, as well as several other surgeries for additional medical problems. I had experienced over 100 hospital stays.

The medications used to treat the disease were also causing some serious side effects. I now had osteonecrosis, a condition where the bones begin to die and become brittle, frequent kidney stones, pancreatitis, and severe bloating and swelling. With all of these maladies flaring up periodically, I often found myself quite ill or hospitalized when holidays came, and Christmas was no exception.

I hated to miss these occasions with my family. We had spent several years watching fireworks from my hospital room window on the 4th of July. And my birthday seemed to be a magnet for trouble! At one point I had spent four birthdays in a row in the hospital. But Christmas was the most difficult to miss. There had been too many of them with me either ending up in the hospital or feeling extremely ill during the holiday. Stress is a major factor with this disease, and I always seemed to push myself too hard with Christmas preparations. I became exhausted, and that was the breeding ground for trouble.

This was one Christmas, I had promised myself and my wife, I would not over-do it and end up in the hospital. We had too many exciting plans for the next two weeks of vacation. This holiday would not be ruined by medical problems!

I could faintly see my wife sleeping in the bed next to me, but she had not stirred yet. We had been up until nearly 3:00 a.m. getting packages wrapped and presents set up for the big morning, and I knew that she would not be in a hurry to rise. I was not so sure our five sons and little daughter would honor such a desire, however. In fact, I was surprised that someone had not already jumped on our bed that morning. I was certain it would not be long now, though.

A yawn pulled me into a stretch, as I once again peered into the wintery morning scene. I could see a crust on the top of the few inches of snow that blanketed our back yard. It seemed almost icy, yet there was still snow falling. It was just what I had hoped for with Christmas morning now here. It didn't seem that it could be Christmas in Idaho without a white blanket stretched across the landscape.

I walked to the bathroom and squinted into the mirror to see what kind of damage my short night's sleep had done to my hair. Though I was considerably bald on top, the hair on each side of my head still managed to get pasted straight out by all of my tossing and turning. I grabbed my brush and tried to mat my remaining hair down with a little water. For a man of 37, I had eluded almost completely a graying to my hair. But, I quickly concluded, it was due to the fact that it seemed to fall out sooner than it could age to the state of gray.

I staggered down the hallway and peeked into each of the bedrooms. Still sleeping. I supposed I could return to bed for another hour or so before the kids would awaken, but I was already so excited for the morning that I wasn't sure I wanted to go back to sleep. It would almost assuredly be one of the most exciting Christmas mornings we had experienced in our home with Nathan just a year old and McKaye, our only daughter, at that merry age of three. Our son, Creed, was now five years of age, while Jared was ready to turn eight. Each was at such a fun stage for Christmas. There would be plenty of squealing and excited chatter when they arose.

Our oldest child, Brock, a quickly growing teenager only days away from his fourteenth birthday, and his younger brother Jordan, nearly eleven, would be the ones having more difficulty wanting to rise early, I figured. Yet, each seemed almost more excited than their younger siblings, wanting to watch their fervor once Santa had come. I appreciated that quality in both of them; each had a wonderful manner with their brothers and sister. Being a teenager had somehow never fazed Brock's enjoyment of children. And Jordan seemed to be following suit. My wife and I had commented regularly about how grateful we had been that Brock was the big brother, with the amazing example he set for his brothers and sister to follow. They respected and loved him, while he clearly adored them; not common for a teenager, but incredibly he seemed to remain oblivious to his good looks and athletic body, too. He instead was so focused on others and his sports that he could not understand why girls were becoming so interested in him.

I headed back to my bedroom and slipped into bed. Perhaps, a little more rest would do me good, I thought. But now, try as I might, I could not get my mind to shut down and allow my body to sleep. I could not quit thinking about the presents that were to be opened soon. I could not stop the flood of adrenaline as I imagined the excitement in my boy's faces when they would see the snowmobile and motorcycle for which I had made a deal. True, they were both pretty old, but they worked. My boys had so enjoyed riding their friends' snowmobiles and motorbikes over the years, that I really wanted to buy them their own. Unfortunately with all of my illnesses and hospital bills, extra money had been almost nonexistent. But this time I had come into an incredible deal. Someone who had owed me some money had now repaid me, and another man had offered me a chance to purchase an older snowmobile and the bike for a great price. I figured regardless of how they looked, as long as they would actually run my boys would be thrilled for such a treasure.

So I made the purchase. I lay wondering who would be most excited. Brock? Jordan? Jared? Or maybe it would be me, full of enjoyment as I watched them trying out the new toys. Yes, that was the way Christmas and giving most often worked; the giver usually received the greater thrill. It was that aspect which made Christmas such a wonderful time to me. People experience feelings of joy and excitement that are seldom felt the rest of the year.

I looked at my watch again. 5:45. Only fifteen minutes had passed. Couldn't morning come just a little sooner on this day? I closed my eyes again and tried to summon sleep. It just didn't seem to want to come. But then…

The next thing I knew, my bed was shaking and the voices of Jared and Creed were echoing in my ear.

"Dad, it's time! I'm sure Santa has come. You guys have to wake up so we can go in!" They knew the law of the household was emphatically stated that no one could pass into our living room, where all of the presents were set, without all of us going together. And it was Mom and Dad first, of course, to set up cameras with which to record the looks of amazement and ecstasy as each child viewed their loot.

I looked at my watch again. Wow! I must have fallen asleep. It was now 6:50 and light had pushed the darkness of the night into ever brighter shades of blue. I feigned exhaustion.

"You must be kidding! Do you know what time it is? Why, we need to sleep another two hours before it's time to get up."

"Oh, Dad! You can't do that to us. It's Christmas! Get up

now before we run into the family room without you!"

"You know the rules," I returned. "Besides, I'm certain Santa has not had time to come yet. We'd better go to sleep for another hour or so."

It seemed to be a ritual that could not be passed by for Dad and Mom to plead for more time to sleep before the grand procession into the world of Christmas. For my wife, Jozet, I think it was truth. But for me, it was all an act. I was more excited than they were for the morning to begin. I only pretended to be a tough customer.

"Dad, you promised that if we stayed in bed until 6:30 that you'd let us get up. It's after 6:30 now. You promised!"

"I'm not sure that your mother is even alive, though, guys. We were up pretty late getting things ready. You better give Mom a little more time."

There was a sudden thud and shaking of the bed. It was Jordan and Brock's bodies crashing on to the mattress.

"Not you, too!" I exclaimed. "You know we'll have to wait for McKaye and Nate to wake up."

"I already woke McKaye up, Dad," Jordan proclaimed. "And Brock is going to go get Nathan out of his crib right now."

"NO, you don't!" yelled Jozet. You guys have to let him sleep as long as he can."

A chorus of "NOs" rang out in the room. I knew it was no use arguing, but Jozet seemed determined to get another half hour. I finally decided I had better start siding with the kids or I may have to wait the additional half hour as well. I didn't want that.

"Jozet, it's no use. I just don't think we're going to be able to have them wait any longer," I said in their defense. Cheers erupted. Jozet smiled. "You are the one who wants to get up. I know you!"

My little charade was history. After nearly sixteen years of marriage I could no longer fool my wife. She knew that I was the biggest kid of them all when it came to Christmas.

"You know that I'm only doing it for these poor, helpless children. I must give them voice. Otherwise, you know that I would much rather sleep," I stated, with all the drama I could muster.

Jozet only laughed. "That will be the day. I know you all too well, dear. You can't con me." She hesitated a moment, then relinquished. "OK, you guys win. I'll get up. But I get a two hour nap this afternoon!"

"Oh, of course," they sang out in unison. "We'll be so quiet that you won't even know we're here," Brock promised, with his arm squared, fingers crossed.

"I see those fingers crossed. The day that you guys are quiet on Christmas, I'll know the world has ended," Jozet chuckled. "Go get Nate up." Cheers filled the air again.

Two tiny legs appeared around the corner. McKaye's long hair was tousled about her shoulders as she rubbed her eyes. "Is it Christmas yet?"

"It is, doll. I have a feeling that Santa Claus has come and brought some presents for you. Do you want to go see?" The smile and happy nod gave a clear reply.

"Everybody get ready to head down the hall, and I want each of you to eat an orange before you start eating any of the candy," Jozet ordered. I smiled. Yes, she was definitely a mother.

"Oh, mom, you can't mean that," Jared protested. "How about I eat some of the chocolate cherries first! That's fruit!" His plea was met with laughs from his brothers, but a quick and absolute "No," from his mother.

Brock walked in the room carrying Nathan. He was still yawning and rubbing the sleep from his eyes. He seemed to somehow comprehend the excitement, regardless of the fact that he was only one year old.

It was now time. I had waited for this day with great anticipation. And I was feeling pretty good, as well. No terrible cramping or vomiting. Although I had not garnered near enough sleep during the night, I was actually feeling well. I could hardly remember the last time I had felt so good on a Christmas morning.

I looked at my children and wife and felt I was a very lucky man at that moment. Each was healthy and happy. And each loved me almost as much as I loved them. What greater present could I have possibly wanted for Christmas? Little did I know the mental pain and anguish each of them would endure as the holiday unfolded. Thank God I didn't know.

"Finally," I thought, with a rush of adrenaline, "It's Christmas morning."

THE MESSAGE

CHAPTER TWO

A Time For Joy...

As each of our children entered the living room there were plenty of shouts of excitement. I was running the camcorder and attempting to preserve the expressions of each elated face for years down the road when we could only watch and reminisce, longing to have those smiling faces at our sides.

We watched with pleasure, but my anticipation was still heightening. Not one of them had seemed to notice the motorcycle and snowmobile helmets sitting under the tree. They were engrossed in the presents which had been laid on their chairs. New games, toys, Barbie dolls, and a weight bench were being carefully examined, but not the helmets. I had been certain Brock or Jordan would notice.

Finally I could wait no longer.

"Hey, guys, what are those things sitting in front of the tree?"

"Well, I imagine those are for you, aren't they, Dad?" Brock replied. Now I understood why they had not given more attention to them.

"No, this is a very special present that Santa and I arranged. It's for you guys."

Jordan's eyes lit up. "For me?"

"For all of you," I said.

"Wow! What is it?" Jordan stepped closer as his brothers each looked on in wonderment. "I know what that is," Jordan continued. "Tyler Wilde's family has some of those. They use them when they ride snowmobiles." The mention of the word brought a sudden gasp of anticipation to each of the boys.

"Do you mean that we get to go on a vacation somewhere and ride some snowmobiles?" Creed yelled.

"Well, maybe. I think you guys better go out to the garage and look around," I said nonchalantly.

It suddenly looked like a stampede of wild buffalo. I heard Jordan yell, "I knew it! I knew it! We got a snowmobile! And a motorcycle!"

The fact that they were beat up and old made absolutely no difference to them. There were hoots and hollers, yells of excitement.

"I can't believe it!" Jared and Brock yelled. "Do they work?" Brock asked.

"They do. But that motorcycle is going to take a little work to get it running very well. The guy who sold them to me assured me that if we couldn't get it going, he would work it over some for us. He's a mechanic," I answered.

"When can we ride them?" Jared impatiently queried.

"Right after we finish opening presents and clean up the family room. I'll come out and ride them with you."

"Oh that's great! But couldn't we just take them for a little ride right now?" Jordan asked.

"I think you might look pretty funny riding them in your pajamas, not to mention that you will probably freeze! No, we need to finish the presents first." My words brought a sigh of dejection, but as their bodies began to chill even in the protection of the garage, they figured I was probably right.

We headed back into the house, determined to open the other packages as quickly as possible. We proceeded to go around the room opening one package at a time until all the presents had been examined and enjoyed. It had been a splendid morning, every bit as exciting as we had anticipated.

A feeling of enjoyment and love seemed to permeate our home. How I wished I could have captured it in my hands and bottled it for future days. The nectar of Christmas is ever so sweet.

THE MESSAGE

CHAPTER THREE

The Accident

It was afternoon before we finally were able to get out to the garage and work on the snowmobile and motorbike. It took only a few pulls and adjustments before the snowmobile was running. It was only minutes more for the boys to figure out how to drive it and head down the road into a vacant field that others had been using for riding as well.

I weighed in my mind whether or not I dared to go riding on the snowmobile with the boys. With a medical history as long as mine, including three major back surgeries, I was concerned about how my back would handle the jarring. The last time I had ridden snowmobiles my left leg had been numb and tingling for a day. I decided to take a short ride, rest for awhile, then assess the damage.

Jozet had gone to the bedroom to catch the two-hour nap we had promised, and the two younger kids had accompanied her. I assured her that I could keep the house quiet with the boys riding their new toys. She thankfully agreed and laid down for a rest.

The wind was biting, with freezing temperatures and snow falling. I was glad that I had purchased the helmet with a good mask designed to keep out the cold and prevent fogging. Each of us had dressed as warmly as possible, but the cold still seemed to penetrate rather easily. With the excitement of the new transports, however, the cold didn't seem to even faze the boys.

I climbed on board the snowmobile and tucked Creed behind me, and told the others that I would take a quick run around the field and be right back.

The snow crunched as the heavy load began to cross it. It was exhilarating to just begin the ride. We crossed the road and headed into the field. Slowly I increased the speed as I could feel my back and legs fairing well. It was great! It had been so long since I had dared to do anything like this, and it felt wonderful. I could imagine the fun the boys and I could have the rest of winter riding this thing.

I headed back and gave the next two a chance to ride, while I took a break to make sure I was still feeling as good as I had originally thought. Every few minutes the snowmobile would pull back up and an exchange of passengers would occur. Everyone was having a blast!

Jordan and Brock then asked me, "Dad, could we try out the motorcycle, too?"

"It's too icy and snowy to ride it now, but we could try to get it going. I've heard that a warm front is moving in next week and we might get a chance to do some riding then."

"That sounds great," they shouted. "Let's go see if we can get it started."

We headed back to the garage and pulled the bike into the open floor space. I sat down on it and gave it a kick to start.

There was no response. Over and over I tried, but there seemed to be no combustion occurring in the engine.

"Dad, can I try it?" Brock asked.

My legs had been significantly weakened through years of surgeries. Brock was an athlete with powerful limbs. He was bound to have better results.

"Sure Brock, give it a try," I said, moving off of the bike.

Time after time he kicked. There was a little gurgle, but that was about it. I could see disappointment beginning to show in the boys' faces.

"Are you sure this thing can run?" Jordan asked. "Maybe it's too old."

"Actually, guys, I saw the man who sold it to me start it up and ride it around his driveway. I'm sure if we make a few adjustments we can get it running. Only problem is, I have no idea how to adjust it. I don't know enough about motorcycles. I guess we'll have to wait until tomorrow and see if we can find someone to help us get it working." That brought a chorus of pleas that I not wait, but find someone to help us now.

"Mr. Wilde could fix it, I bet," Jordan rang out. "I'm sure he'd be happy to help us get it going. Besides I wanted to get Tyler to come over and ride snowmobiles with me."

"Alright," I said. "I could call him and see if he has a minute to look at it." Jordan dashed to get the phone. I hated to bother Lawry Wilde on Christmas day, but he was always so willing to give help when anyone needed it. I decided that it might be alright.

I took the phone from Jordan and dialed the number. Lawry was happy to assist us. He lived down the street from us, so he came over immediately.

As I watched Lawry working on the bike, I wished I had learned more about mechanics. He seemed so at home with each part of the bike and its engine.

"It's too bad I am so inept at this kind of stuff," I confessed to Lawry.

"It just takes some time being around these machines," he replied.

"In my case, I'm afraid it would take more than just being around them. My wife is the handyman around our house."

"That's because you're always sick! If I were sick as much as you are, I wouldn't get anything done."

His remarks were kind, but I knew there was some truth to them as well. I had been blessed to be able to keep going considering my medical portfolio. I had experienced incredible pain in my fight with the Crohn's disease and its side effects. Often I had endured bowel obstructions, caused by the intestines hardening and constricting. These were extremely painful. Altogether, I had spent many years, often months at a time, in hospitals enduring treatments to re-open the obstructed intestines, or having surgery to remove diseased sections in them. There had been a few close calls, flirting with death it seemed. But with God's blessings, and some excellent medical assistance, I had been able to come out on top each time. Sometimes I wondered, though, if the pain would ever end.

My health problems had also made it extremely difficult to work, forcing me to start my own business to try to support my family. The medical bills had been a nightmare. It seemed impossible to ever dig out of the financial hole we were in. Jozet had been good to help by teaching dance and gymnastics, and by the grace of God, we had somehow continued to survive.

My immune system had been wiped out by the medications and chemo therapies used to control the disease. This made me very susceptible to every bug that came around. Each morning as I took my truckload of vitamins and medications, I wondered how my body ever continued to function.

And the setbacks were always a major obstacle. Every time I would get a work project going, my body would break down again. Then it would be back to the hospital, another few weeks of tests, intense pain, and treatments, then recovery. By that time, all the momentum would be gone for the project. I would try to regroup and start over. Sometimes I felt like I was running a race, and someone would continually place a hurdle in my lane just a little too late for me to avoid crashing into it. It became a little bit tougher to rise each time I fell, realizing the other runners had long since passed me.

The lessons from my years in athletics became a driving force for me. I had been taught by my parents from the time I was a child never to give up. I remembered football games, wrestling matches, basketball games, and more, where the key to the victory had been the inner drive to endure to the end. It was a major piece to the formula for success.

Though I had been involved in many sports, I enjoyed football the most. In my senior year of high school I had been named to one All-American team, and had numerous colleges contact me about possibly playing football for them. This was a most exciting time for me. Two of the legendary coaches of football, LaVell Edwards of BYU and Bill Parcells of Air Force (who later became the Super Bowl champion coach of the New York Giants), recruited me. I could hardly believe it. I had worked years for this day and it had finally arrived. I could not have been more excited.

But then life took a terrible turn. I was injured in a weightlifting accident, rupturing two discs in my back. Before I ever played on a college football field, I had to have an emergency surgery or face being paralyzed. I would never play football again.

I was devastated. For some time I felt as if my world had collapsed, everything I had worked for destroyed. It took great effort from deep inside to pull myself together and realize there would be other dreams. For a young man only eighteen years of age it was a most difficult trial to endure. But God used it as a teaching experience for my future.

As badly as that experience of losing my college scholarship had hurt, I now deeply appreciated the lessons I had learned. They had given me strength to endure the roller coaster of pain and emotions of the last eighteen years. I could see them now as a blessing, though the stretching of my soul had seemed so unpleasant.

I recognized that athletics is an amazing preparation for life. There had been many times when teams I had been on had to find the will and determination to continue when the odds seemed insurmountable, and often we had won. I had learned how to deal with the disappointment of a season-ending injury. I had learned how to play with pain. I had learned to never, ever, give up. Learning to rise each time I fell became an incredible tool needed for my future.

I had no idea at that moment how important each of those lessons would be in the next couple of months. Thank God we are not allowed to see the future. How often we would seek to change the course, not realizing the need for such opposition.

I watched Lawry as he adjusted the engine. His skills were evident. Within a few minutes he had the bike running. The boys cheered knowing the bike was actually able to function. It was now a reality.

Lawry drove the bike in a circle in the driveway. It coughed and sputtered as he pulled back into the garage.

"I think it needs a little more adjusting." He swung his leg off the bike and leaned down and quickly made another adjustment.

"Dad, can I ride it?" Jordan asked.

"I think we'd better get it working a little better before you try it."

Lawry stood and brushed off his pants. "Actually I think I'm finished. Lance, why don't you drive it down the driveway and see what you think. I believe I have it working about right now."

I was anxious to see how it felt to ride again and quickly positioned myself on the seat. I had no idea as I pulled out of the garage that I was beginning, perhaps, the wildest ride of my life.

There was a thin layer of snow on my driveway, mostly flakes which had fallen in the last ten hours. I cautiously drove down the driveway with no intention of trying to build up any speed. As I came to the end of the cement, I turned into the road. Not a sound could be heard in the neighborhood except for two of the boys riding the snowmobile in the field, and the purr and coughing of the motorbike. I imagined most of our neighbors were enjoying the restfulness of a Christmas afternoon.

My speed could not have been more than five to seven miles per hour as I began to turn the bike to head back to the garage. It didn't look very icy, but I clearly misjudged.

As I began to turn, the bike began to slide sideways to the left. I reached out my right leg in an effort to catch myself. The surface of the road, however, was too slick, and the bike continued its slide with my left leg hooked around it. I felt a snap as I crashed to the asphalt. The bike slid out from under my left leg.

Pain rushed into my legs and lower back. I knew instantly my back was in trouble. I felt the familiar sharp sciatic pain shooting down my left leg and into my foot. I recognized that feeling all too well from my former back injuries. It had taken three major surgeries over the years to try to stabilize my lower back. It had improved significantly over the years, but I could clearly discern that I had re-injured my lower spine.

I now felt a gush of sciatic pain heading down my right leg, as well. I had never had much pain in my right leg from the former back injuries. This was new, and disturbed me.

I decided to attempt to turn onto my side. If I passed that test, I thought, I would endeavor to stand. As I made my first effort to move I felt a heaviness in my right side. It wouldn't even begin to rise as I tried to turn. I knew instantly something was seriously wrong.

There was significant pain, but I imagine shock was masking the full intensity of it at that moment.

Lawry raced over to me. The older boys had run down to the field to tell the others that the motorcycle actually was running.

"Are you alright?" Lawry asked.

"I don't think so. I can feel there is something definitely wrong. I can't move at all."

"Oh, man, Lance, I should've never let you get on that bike with your health."

"Hey, it wasn't your fault. I'm the one who chose to ride it. I would have ridden it to check it out even if you hadn't asked me. Don't you feel responsible."

He looked unconvinced.

"Listen," I tried to assure him further, "who would have thought that riding a bike at that speed could hurt anyone! I'm just a wimp!"

"No, you just have too many health problems. I should have thought." He paused in thought for a moment. "Do you think if I helped you we could get you to your house? I could get my truck and we could lift you into it."

"Let's try it," I said. "I don't know whether I can do it, but we should try."

Lawry put his arm under my shoulder and began to lift. "No!" I yelled out in pain. "Something is broken. I can feel it."

"Do you want me to go get Jozet?" he asked. I thought of all the plans we had made for the Christmas vacation. I knew it was serious enough that I would not be getting around for a few days at the least. I imagined she would be thinking, just as we were now, "Why in the world were you riding a motorcycle in this weather with your health problems?" That was a question I knew I could not answer satisfactorily. I had not meant to go riding; just to test the bike out on a little jaunt. But I knew my answer was hollow.

"If you want to save my life, Lawry, don't tell my wife! She'll kill me before I ever die from the injuries!" I said, laughingly.

"Probably me, too," Lawry insisted.

"No, I'm the klutz that's always getting hurt. I should have never gotten on that thing. I can't blame her if she does shoot me!"

Lawry informed me that he was going to go call an ambulance for me and ran down the street to his home. I was lying right in the middle of the road, so I was glad that it was such a quiet street. I kept looking each way to see if any cars were going to come, though luckily none did.

One of my neighbors ran out to the road. "Lance, what happened?"

"Oh, you know me. What a klutz! I fell off this little motorbike and I am pretty sure I've broken something. I can't move."

"Oh, no! Should I go get your wife?"

"To tell you the truth, I wish she didn't have to know, but I'm certain I'm not going to be able to hide this one. I guess you'd better. Thanks."

They ran towards my house, as I lay trying to come up with the best story of my life. Nothing seemed to come to mind. All I could think of was how disappointed Jozet would be. We had gone through so many difficult years of health problems together. There were enough surgeries and emergency room visits inherent in my illness. I didn't need to invent new ways to land in the hospital. I could only imagine what she would say when she heard that I was riding the motorcycle.

My uncle is an orthopedic surgeon, and he had shared plenty of horror stories of healthy people being broken up, or even killed, riding "those things".

I heard the crunching of snow and looked up to see Lawry running back to me. "I've called the ambulance and it should be here any minute."

"Thanks for all your help, Lawry," I said. I could see in his eyes he was still feeling guilty. I was just beginning to try to assure him once again he need not feel responsible, when I saw the face of one of my sons peek out of the field and look down to see me lying in the road. "Oh, man, my kids are going to really be upset."

"Let me go get them for you." He began to walk toward the field when I saw the ambulance lights flashing as it turned the corner toward me. They were like a magnet. Several of my neighbors must have seen the lights as well, and came to find out what had happened. Each was so concerned and wanted to do anything they could to help. Two of them grabbed the bike out from the middle of the road and told me that they would take it back into my garage.

As the paramedics began to open the back end and pull out the long white stretcher, I heard the crunch of footsteps approaching my head. I turned to look and saw my neighbor approaching with my wife. One look at her face told me that any hopes I had for sympathy were pure fantasy. I tried to smile.

"What were you doing, Lance?" Jozet asked, with a tone that could have cut ice.

"I was just trying to see if this bike worked."

"With YOUR health?!" I had no answer for that, so I was only too glad to have the paramedic interrupt our discussion.

"Tell me you weren't riding a motorcycle and did this," the paramedic stated emphatically. Now things were really getting unfair. My wife on one side, and a paramedic agreeing with her on the other.

"Well, not really. I was only going five miles per…"

"What've we got here?" another paramedic had walked over with the gurney. "Someone trying to hot-dog it on a motorcycle in the snow?"

"No. See…"

A third paramedic swung the gurney's other end around, "You really wouldn't be dumb enough to rip around in the snow, would you?"

"Listen, I…"

Then the police showed up, and I was certain the same questions and looks of disbelief would continue. So, I just stopped talking and tried to ignore the pain that was ripping through my back.

It was then that two of my sons arrived. Tears were already streaming down their faces. That tore at me more than any of the physical pain or mental discomfort I was feeling. I knew how disappointed they would be, but even more, they were forever having to say goodbye to me as I would be driven, in terrible pain, to the hospital. This time, though, the vehicle was not driven by our family or friends. The flashing lights and paramedics stated unequivocally to their minds that something was very seriously wrong. It was the first time we had ever required an ambulance.

I tried to calm their fears. So did Jozet. They didn't seem to hear our words, however. The lights from the ambulance and visage of the paramedics and policeman were overpowering to their minds.

I was being placed into the back of the ambulance when I saw my two older sons coming out of the field. I could see a look of shock on their faces. One of the paramedics informed Jozet that they would like her to come to the hospital to complete the paperwork and reports. Several of the neighbors immediately offered to watch the kids until she could get back.

I wanted so badly to talk with my other boys before the ambulance began to pull away, but the paramedics wanted to get us going. I could only see their faces from the back of the van. Kind-hearted neighbors sought to explain to the boys what had happened. I know I will never forget that scene as I gazed into my four sons' faces full of fears and tears.

As they closed the back doors, I silently thought to myself, "If I could only move the hands of time back a short thirty minutes." If I could only dry the tears of my four frightened sons.

CHAPTER FOUR

Happy New Year?

Voices faded in and out as I began to awake. The smell of alcohol preps, the faint ringing in my ears, and the slightly bitter taste left from the anesthesia and tubes that had been placed in my mouth, gave me an immediate understanding of where I was. I had experienced these sensations all too many times. The sounds, smells, and feelings of the surgical recovery room were very familiar to me, and I was deeply thankful to have lived through yet another surgery.

"Lance, can you hear me?" the recovery room nurse asked as she checked my blood pressure again.

"Yes." The voices of the nurses around me were still fuzzy, but I was cognizant enough to recognize their words.

"Lance, do you know where you are?"

"Yes. I'm in the recovery room." It took much strength just to form each of those words and speak. The voices of the nurses were familiar. I was still too groggy to discern who each nurse was, but I was certain that they had worked on me in other surgeries.

"Did they replace my hip?" I asked, remembering my conversation with the doctor just before I drifted to sleep from the anesthesia. Doctor Stan Griffiths, the orthopaedic surgeon who had been on call for Christmas Day, informed me that he was planning to replace my hip in the surgery.

"I am not sure, Lance. I haven't read the surgical report."

The more I awoke the more I could feel the pain intensifying in my right hip and lower back. The sciatic pain I had felt immediately after the fall was still present. The pain in my hip had greatly increased with the surgical procedure that had been performed.

"Could I get some pain medication? My hip is really hurting," I asked.

"I am giving you some IV medication right now, Lance. You should be able to feel the relief in a minute."

I had not even finished saying, "Thank you," before I began to drift back to sleep with the relaxation the pain medication brought to my body. It was a most welcomed sleep.

The next thing I new I was waking up in my hospital room with most of my family gathered around me. I asked what day it was.

"It's late in the evening of Christmas Day, honey," my mother responded. Mom and Dad had come to the hospital as soon as they had heard of my accident. They had waited with me in hospitals much longer than anyone should have had to in nine lifetimes. But they never complained. Mom had endured many health problems, herself, so she was able to understand my pain in a way that few others could.

As I slowly became more awake, I wished that somehow two or three days had passed without me noticing, for I knew, all too well, what I would feel in the coming days.

The pains of the first few hours after returning from the recovery room are always some of the most difficult. This time was no exception. The slightest bumping of the bed, the noises in the room; it all brought additional discomfort. And, due to the multitude of surgeries and hospital stays I had endured, the pain medication didn't have great effect on me. So, it was a game of endurance, with the never ending hope of sleep.

Jozet sat at the edge of my bed, her hand on my forehead dabbing it with a damp cloth. My father had begun to rub the bottoms of my feet. He knew how much this seemed to help me when I was in considerable pain.

"What did they end up doing in the surgery?" I asked. "Did they replace my hip?"

"No," Dad informed me. "They were going to, but decided that with the position of the fracture, it might be better to pin it. They pinned it back together with four long screws. The doctor felt you would recover quicker this way."

I groaned. I had heard so many people tell me that they have fewer problems down the road with a hip replacement. I hated to hear that news, even though the type of surgery I had undergone was less invasive.

I looked at Jozet, still trying to help relieve my pain with the cool washcloth. "I am so sorry, dear, for all of this. I know it has ruined our Christmas vacation."

"It's alright, Lance. Don't worry about it. We are all going to be just fine. We can just be very thankful that it wasn't something worse."

Her words brought me comfort. I could see that she had forgiven me for my "ride". As the two of us traveled in the back of the ambulance to the hospital, she had expressed her anger for my lack of thought. I tried to help her understand that I had never intended to go riding, but only to test out the bike. I really had not believed that traveling so slowly could cause such an accident.

As we had waited in the emergency room for the doctors to determine what the diagnosis and prognosis would be, she seemed to slowly lose her resolve to "have me tortured." I believe she finally decided the pain she was witnessing me endure might be sufficient for my repentance process.

I looked at her now, sitting at the side of my bed, and realized how difficult these hospital stays had become. The pain in her eyes spoke volumes of what each new problem meant to her life. I quickly felt compassion for her and an understanding of why she had reacted the way she did earlier that day. My thought was about the Christmas vacation time together we would now miss. Her thought was of the husband and father that she would miss, and the multitude of other implications that carried. She had exhibited the Christ-like characteristic of "long-suffering" for so many years, through countless medical tragedies and disasters, and she was reaching her limit. I felt ashamed for not having understood her feelings better.

"We'll make it through this, Jozet, together. Believe me, I

never meant to do something stupid. I never thought this could happen. I am really sorry."

She nodded, as tears filled her eyes. And for a moment, my pain was lightened as I immersed myself in understanding someone else's pain; a profound truth I would soon learn in powerful quantity.

Jozet had to leave to get back to our children, but Mom and Dad, along with many other family and friends, sat with me the rest of the night. I was in too much pain to talk, but it was comforting just to have them with me.

I remember waking up nearly every thirty minutes that night. The pain was intense enough that I could hardly manage sleep, but my level of fatigue thankfully drove me into slumber ever so often.

When I awoke on the morning of the 26th, I was informed that my regular physician, Dr. Kenneth Krell, would be around to see me soon. He knew my problem of weak and porous bones better than anyone. I was certain that he, too, would have many of the same probing questions to ask me of why I had been riding a motorcycle. I decided I could make it through one more embarrassing interview.

I had plenty of questions to ask as well. I was already wanting to know how quickly I could get out of the hospital and when I would be fully mobile again. Some of these questions were better meant for Dr. Griffiths. But he had left to do some mountain climbing for the next couple of weeks, so I waited patiently for Dr. Krell to visit me.

I had met Dr. Krell soon after having been diagnosed with Crohn's Disease, nearly eighteen years earlier. He had been new in town, and was pretty new in his practice, as well. He seemed to know Crohn's Disease better than any other doctor I had met, however. Over the eighteen years he had treated me hundreds of times, and I had developed a great trust, respect, and friendship for him, as well as his partner, Dr. Douglas Wattmore, who had later joined him and treated me frequently, as well. We had lived in several other places around the country, but kept coming home so that we could be near these competent and dedicated physicians. We had not been sorry.

"Lance, what in the world were you doing riding a motorcycle in the snow and ice?" I heard from Doctor Krell as he approached. He didn't even need to say a word for me to know it was him approaching my room. There was a familiar click and cadence to his walk that I could hear as he came down the hall. I was already trying to decide how to answer that question better than I had answered it during the last 24 hours.

"Just tell me that what I have heard isn't true," he continued. I turned my head so that I could see him. Dr. Krell stood about five feet seven inches tall, with curly brown hair and medium build. His stature was not that imposing, but his manner and words drew immediate respect. His face this morning, thankfully, conveyed a smile for me, even though his questions penetrated to my guilt-ridden heart.

"There is more to the story than you have been told, I am sure!" I replied with a sense of great earnestness.

"Alright, I'm listening. What happened?" I started at the beginning and shared the full story, seeking to reassure him that I had not taken complete leave of my senses. He was kind, even though I knew that he, along with my wife, wanted to have that motorcycle destroyed forever.

After doing a complete physical, he asked me if I had been fighting with any cold symptoms lately.

"Yes, I guess. But only a little. Why?"

"Oh, it's nothing at the moment, but it sounds a bit tight in your lungs. We had better get some x-rays and make sure that we don't have some pneumonia developing." He patted me on the arm, then said as he was leaving, "I'd bet Jozet wasn't too happy to hear about this one!"

I smiled. "You got that one right. I'm lucky I'm not dead from spousal inflicted injuries!" He chuckled, then headed back down the hall.

I pondered what Dr. Krell had said. I had not felt any tightness in my lungs, but he was always so quick to pick up any abnormalities. I had a feeling there was something more significant than a cold brewing.

Later that afternoon the nurses and physical therapists came into my room and informed me that it was time to stand and walk a few paces. I was amazed that it was possible to begin so soon after the surgery. But it honestly felt good to get up and move. I definitely felt some pain, but I faired far better than I had anticipated.

Day two of my recovery was not what we had hoped it would

be. I was developing a chest cough and was beginning to have more and more difficulty breathing. The reports from the radiologist were not positive, either. They stated that extensive infiltrates, or foreign matter, along with possible "fatty emboli," were beginning to gather in both lungs and block off the air passages. Something serious was developing quickly. It was certain that I had developed pneumonia. And now I was beginning to cough up small blood clots, as well. This signified more severe problems.

Dr. Krell ordered more tests and hooked me up to oxygen through a small tube in the nose. We would closely watch the development and hope for no further progression of the clots and other infiltrates.

I spent the rest of the day visiting with family and friends in my hospital room and watching a few football bowl games on TV. I was pleased that at least my hip was improving a little.

Day three of recovery is always expected to be something of a setback. So it was more the type of setbacks which occurred that intensified our fears, for they didn't seem related to my hip. I was struggling more and more to get oxygen. The results of the new set of x-rays confirmed the continuing spread of the infiltrates, and that fluid was filling in my lungs.

The oxygen rate was increased again, and I had to begin carrying an oxygen tank with me every time I attempted to walk, even if only a few feet away.

X-rays were now being taken more than once per day, and reports were immediately called to the hospital nursing floor.

Other signs were becoming serious as well. The white blood cell count was skyrocketing, which clearly indicated an infection. A fever had started, and my temperature had risen to103 degrees. At night it was becoming so difficult to breathe, that I feared dying in my sleep.

On New Year's Eve, after having friends and family visit in an effort to give me some semblance of celebration, I fell asleep in absolute exhaustion. I began to dream that I was suffocating. My mind suddenly recognized there was truth mixed in with the dream and aroused me from sleep. As I awoke, I quickly realized I had somehow pulled the oxygen tube out of my nose. There was no outside oxygen flowing into my body. My lungs were now so blocked that I could not obtain adequate oxygen on my own to survive. I wrenched and gasped, seeking with every ounce of strength to obtain enough air to supply my body's needs. A monitor next to me gave a continual reading of the oxygen saturation level in the blood. A normal person would register at 95-100%. Anything under 90% was a problem. As I looked to the monitor, the reading showed 47%! I was so weak and starved for air that I had great difficulty finding the tube to get it back in my nose. I suddenly remembered my button to call the nurse, and pushed for help. I knew, though, that unless they somehow knew it was an emergency, it could be fifteen to thirty minutes before someone would come.

I began praying for strength to find the tube and get it back in my nose. I was struggling so desperately to breathe, however, that my hands were shaking dramatically. After what felt like an eternity, I finally located the oxygen tube and brought it back into position. Though it was instant help, for the first few minutes it felt as if I were trying to breath through a tiny straw!

About that time a nurse pushed open my door and asked me what was needed. He quickly discerned my problem and promptly turned the oxygen on full force. I drank in the oxygen as if my parched tongue was in need of water and someone had turned a flood into my mouth. I had never fought so long and hard for air, nor had I ever been so thankful for the quick relief.

I thanked my nurse and explained to him what had happened. Together we taped the tube onto my nose so that it could not pull loose again. My nurse then assured me that he would check on me every few minutes to make certain it did not occur again.

The next day, New Year's Day, Jozet and I pondered the new developments. My overall situation was becoming markedly worse. Each x-ray and test done on my lungs were showing more and more blockage of the air passage, and the white blood cell count was continuing to rise. I had pneumonia and had become extremely anemic, as well. Blood transfusions were begun to help stabilize this problem. On top of all that, different cultures were showing more infections were developing. It was difficult to determine what could be causing these new problems. We were becoming significantly more concerned, as were my doctors. These were not the kind of New Year's presents we had hoped for.

The doctors changed my oxygen tubing to a full mask that could infuse greater amounts of oxygen. This seemed to make a real difference for a day or two, but soon I was losing the battle again. With the hospital full, there was only so much the nurses could do to watch me. We started having a family member or friend sleep in a cot beside me. We didn't feel that we could take a chance of me somehow losing the oxygen mask again.

The next two nights in a row, it happened again. We could not understand how I was able to get the taped tube off of my mask in the middle of my sleep, but I did. A buzzer on the monitor would squeal if the oxygen saturation level dropped below 90%. When the buzzer would go off, then my companion would awaken to quickly give me assistance. Thankfully it worked, but we still were not winning the war. I could not breathe without the oxygen running at a full rate at all times. And even then, I was feeling like I was starving for air.

The next day, Dr. Whattmore, (Dr. Krell's partner) met with us for a short conference. He shared with us the updated results from tests and explained that they were deeply concerned about the possibilities that I had developed a rare lung disease called ARDS (Adult Respiratory Distress Syndrome). They believed it was possibly being caused by small amounts of bone marrow escaping from the fractured hip and passing through the blood stream into the lungs. He tried to assure us that this was not conclusive yet, but that if it was correct, it was a most serious condition. Statistics show the majority of patients who contract ARDS die from it. If we were to win this battle, we would have to be very aggressive.

It was decided I needed more immediate attention. I was

moved to Intermediate Care. We hoped we could gain control of the infections, diseases, and continually developing problems in my lungs. It was now January 7, 1999. I had been in the hospital nearly two weeks already. Within a few short days, however, the battle of my life would begin.

CHAPTER FIVE

Begging For Breath

It was now Sunday, January 10th. My son, Jordan, had been sitting with me that morning. Because of the problems I had been experiencing with my breathing, we always had someone with me. My older boys really enjoyed spending some time with me. I greatly appreciated it, as well.

About mid-morning, however, things began to get really bad. I was having a harder and harder time breathing, to the point that I was sucking as hard as I could to get enough air to feel any comfort.

About that time, one of the doctors came in and checked me. I could see from his reaction that things were serious, but with my son there he didn't want to exhibit too much concern.

Something inside me was telling me that things were very unstable, and that I needed to get my family up to my room. I knew that my wife was at church, along with the rest of our children, as were my parents. My brother, Mark, however, lived in another area and would be attending a church that convened at a different time. So I called him.

I tried to turn my head far enough to the side that Jordan could not hear me, but by the look on his face when I hung up, he had heard part of my words. I had hoped the noise of the TV and the pumps would be sufficient to drowned out my voice while I was speaking, but it had not.

I had told Mark I felt very seriously like I was dying, and that the doctor had just been in and seemed to show some of the same fear. They were discussing the possibility of rushing me into surgery if things got any worse. I asked Mark to please go get Jozet and inform the rest of the family. He said he would be on his way immediately.

The minutes seemed to pass like hours as I fought for air. It was killing me to look into the eyes of my son and see the fear that was building.

"Dad, are you going to be alright?" Jordan asked with eyes filled with tears.

"Oh, I hope so. Pray for me. Heavenly Father will do something to help us, I'm sure," I said, each word punctuated with a raspy gasp. I spoke in an effort to reassure myself as well as my son. I had experienced so many horrible medical situations over the past twenty years, I was used to having to fight hard to live. But, without a doubt, my body was telling me this time was different.

I thought back on the multitude of miracles I had seen occur through the many years of intense physical trial and summoned all the faith I could to my mind. As I recalled some of the most life threatening situations, when God had preserved me through the hands of competent physicians, and literal miracles, I was able to gain faith, though each desperate breath was telling me I could not live much longer.

I looked at Jordan. I would give anything to stay here with my boys and watch them grow up. Tears began to fill my eyes as I thought of the incredible and almost indescribable love I had for that boy. I wanted to wipe away his tears and fears, and hold him.

I reached out and took his hand into my swollen fingers and caressed the back of it.

"Jordan, I love you. I love you so much. No matter what happens, don't give up. Don't give up on me. Somehow I know I'll be back, regardless of how bad it looks. Do you understand me?"

Tears were flowing down his cheeks now. I watched my ten year old boy turn into a young man in that short moment. He summoned every bit of courage he possessed as he sought to swallow his urge to cry, and said, "OK, Dad. I'll remember." I pulled him close and gave him a hug that I knew might have to last for a long time. Then I turned over and began my fight.

It wasn't much longer before Mark came into my room. It was such a relief for me to have him there to comfort and assure Jordan. I needed him, too. I could feel things slipping fast.

I wanted to be able to see Jozet again before anything serious occurred, but I didn't know if I could hold on that long. Apparently I did, but I was too near unconsciousness to remember.

What I do remember was this. The alarm was sounding; I was gasping. Once again I was struggling to get enough air and felt that I was suffocating. But this time it was much more intense.

I began to feel panicky. My hands were tingling. Sweat was

cascading down my face as if in a sauna. The room seemed to be spinning. I was getting more and more dizzy and extremely nauseated. All I could do was fight for air and pray to God for help.

I had never quite realized how absolutely crucial oxygen is to our survival. And at that moment I would have given anything to be able to calmly expand my lungs and take in their fill. But I could not. Try as hard as I might, my lungs had become so full of clots, infections, abscesses, and disease that I could not suck in enough air to function. The sensation was terrifying. And the conclusion would be most certain if I did not obtain help immediately.

Mark raced down the hall to obtain help for me.

I turned my head and looked at the oxygen gauge to see if it was running full force. It was. I remember turning to look to my doorway to see if anyone was coming to help. That was the last thing I saw before everything suddenly went black.

Pitch black. A thicker, darker blackness I had never seen. It seemed as if it came from nowhere, yet immediately filled everywhere and everything. I could see nothing. And this all transpired so quickly that I was taken completely by surprise. My immediate thought was, "Who turned off my light!"

I stood and began to walk in this palpable darkness towards where, I thought, must be the light switch. I put my arms directly in front of me and pushed forward, feeling to the right, then left to find the switch. I suddenly realized that I was walking under my own power, and, curiously, there was no more pain. Just a moment before I was wrenching in agony, and now I felt...nothing. Nothing but thick, inky darkness.

CHAPTER SIX

A Most Glorious Abode

As I stepped forward I pushed outward in the darkness and brushed against something. It felt much like a thin veil or curtain. As I parted the substance, an intense light filled with warmth and love fell upon me and beckoned me forward. It was a brilliant light that immediately dispersed all the darkness about me. It was soothing and satisfying. It carried a peace that I wanted to embrace. Deep inside me it felt somehow familiar; a feeling from deep within that was sweet to my soul. I stepped forward into the light.

Though as yet I had not come to a realization of where I was, I instantly perceived I was entering into a most magnificent dimension or sphere which far surpassed the beauty of any place I had ever visited. The peace was consuming and the beauty transcending.

"Where am I?" I thought to myself. "What has happened to me? Wasn't I just fighting for my very…life!" An awareness of my true location was suddenly permeating my mind. I suddenly felt anxious, not knowing what I might see or what might happen.

Immediately in front of me stretched a lush lawn of emerald hue, yet mixed with a combination of sky-blue. I had never seen such a vibrant, brilliant color. Trees could be seen in numerous places around the landscape. They, too, were much more impressive than anything I had ever seen. Leaves and sprigs carried varieties of color such as crimson, gold, blazing yellows of fire, shades of green and blue, and deep blood-red. One stem may have numerous flowers of different variety and color. These flowers and shrubbery cast soft and deep tones of warmth and splendor, as if mixed by a master painter. I was enthralled with the beauty which encompassed me.

Before me, scattered around the lawn and trees, were numerous people grouped in small clusters, some sitting together under trees reading and having discussions, others grouped in intent discourse or thought.

Suddenly I felt someone approaching me from behind. I turned to behold the faces of some of my closest relatives. In the front of the group was my cousin, Randy McMillan, who had died nearly 20 years earlier, from leukemia. He looked great! He had been a state champion wrestler in high school, and had gone on to college to continue his career. He had been full of life and ready to take on the world when he contracted this deadly disease and died. His stature now, however, was every bit as powerful as I had ever remembered him appearing, definitely not the sickly young man that I had known at his death. And his keen sense of humor appeared to be every bit intact. He stepped toward me and greeted me with a warm embrace.

"Lance, it's so good to see you! We've been looking forward to your arrival!" Randy's words caught me by surprise. They had known I was coming.

"It's wonderful to see you, as well. But your words confuse me. If you knew I was coming, then am I really...permanently...dead?" I asked, not certain that I wanted to have my life completed.

"We'll talk about that later. These other family members want to get re-acquainted with you, too," he said, pointing to the others standing in the group with us.

One by one they stepped forward toward me and introduced themselves. There was my Dad's father, Grandpa Mark Richardson, and his wife, Grandma Mary Richardson, Uncle Howard (Randy's father), Great Grandpa Charles Edmund Richardson, and several others.

I had not seen my Grandpa Mark since I was about three years old. All I remembered of him was an old, sickly, haggard man. He had been very ill before his death. But here he was now before me, a very good-looking young man. He looked to be about 25-30 years of age, what many would consider to be one's prime. Though he looked so different I still recognized him immediately.

"Oh, Grandpa, it is so good to see you."

"It's great to see you, Lance. We've been anxiously awaiting your visit." He stepped back and took a long look at me. "You look good! I can see your Dad's characteristics in you. I've enjoyed helping you and your family so much over the past years."

I appreciated his assessment. But his final sentence caught

my interest. "What do you mean by that, Grandpa? How have you helped us?"

"Oh, Lance, you'd be surprised how involved many of us are in your lives," he responded. "It's really quite exciting. We'll show you more about how it works in awhile."

Randy looked at me with a smile. "In most cases, Lance, when you pray to God for help, it is your dead relatives and loved ones who are sent by God to help you in answer to your prayers. Thus we weld links and bonds of love within the family forever. The family is the central and eternal unit of our society." His words carried a powerful feeling of truth. It felt so right! Who would love you more, and desire to help you more, than your family and closest friends!

"And so, those relatives of yours who have lived righteous lives can be used as ministering servants, by God, to assist His children who are still in mortality. We serve you, and you serve us. It is the mode of Heaven."

"That is so incredible," I said. "It's as if they are angels sent to help us."

"Yes, it is." Randy agreed.

Each of the words he had shared conveyed such meaning and clarity. I understood completely. And then it occurred to me. Randy had spoken these truths to me, but not with his mouth and audible voice. He had spoken to my mind. Until that moment, each of my relatives had spoken to me using their mouths. But not now. Randy's last statements were made to me with his mind.

Instantly, I heard my Grandfather's voice in my mind saying to me, "We do not need to speak with our mouths. We have done so to make this change somewhat easier for you. We can speak to you spirit to spirit. And by speaking spirit to spirit, we are able to communicate much more completely. Thus, you are now experiencing my message to you with multiple senses, not only with your ears."

It was true. I had not only heard his words with my spirit and in my mind, but I had experienced them in a most wonderful way. It seemed as if I had absorbed these words. And at the same time as the words came into my mind, I saw a picture of what he was telling me. I felt the emotions he desired to communicate to me, as well. I understood on a higher level than I ever had before.

"Wow! This is amazing!" I said, using my mouth to speak back to them. "Can I speak to you in that manner, as well?"

"You did before this life. When you lived as a spirit before you were born into mortality, you had many talents and capabilities that you have now forgotten. In time, these will come back to your memory. For the moment, though, don't worry about it," Randy explained.

From that time on they alternated in speaking via mouth and by spirit. I could see that often they would do things in a manner to make me feel more comfortable with my new surroundings. I appreciated their efforts, but was also deeply interested in seeing how their world operated and functioned. The communication process was one of the most impressive to me.

Throughout the remainder of my experience in their realm I would see, hear, feel, and internalize the messages given to me when communicated spirit to spirit.

As I looked around me, the beauty seemed almost indescribable. "Oh, how I would love to have my family see all of this with me," I thought. Yes, they were still very present in my mind. In fact, at that moment, my heart ached, as it were, to reunite with them. I was still not certain whether or not I had ended my life for good. Something inside me told me that it was not over, though logic concluded otherwise. Yet, with friends and relatives whom I loved so much present to greet me, I closed my eyes and basked for a second in the incredible peace that permeated every fibre of my being. It felt as if I were being wrapped in the arms of my mother. No, it was even more than that. It was if I were in the arms of my...*maker*. "That is it!" I suddenly recognized. "That is why it feels so familiar."

At that moment, I was once again wrapped in the love of my God; yet the feelings inside me spoke that He was more than that. The spirit inside me gave me understanding beyond all that I had ever known. God indeed was my *Father*. I was his *son*. He was my *Heavenly Father*. He was my *Creator*, and more than that. He loved me as much as I love each of my children, but even more perfectly. I knew it and comprehended it completely at that moment. I felt the truth surge through my spirit just as blood courses through a mortal's veins."

I thought back to that moment only hours earlier when I had looked into the eyes of my son and felt an intensity of love beyond any love I had felt. It was this kind of love my God, my Father, had for me.

Then my memory went further. The whole plan of life was a pattern of our former life in heaven. I had heavenly parents. There was indeed a Father, and most certainly a Mother, in heaven who loved me.

I remembered them at that moment. It was sacred. And the love was so consuming, I felt I would never want to leave again. And though I had not known it were possible until that moment, I cried. Yes, I was home again.

THE MESSAGE

CHAPTER SEVEN

Waiting and Wondering

As I continued on in the most incredible learning experience of my life, my family was experiencing the awful reality of my possible death. After I had recovered, my wife and family related to me the difficult circumstances through which they passed "while I was sleeping".

Jozet received word of my precarious condition while sitting in church. My brother Mark had knocked on the door of the church classroom to find her. She turned to see him beckoning her to come out into the hall.

Jozet had just finished telling some of our friends and neighbors how I was finally doing somewhat better. It was a bit of a shock to see Mark at the door. His being there could only signify one thing; bad news. She was not ready to hear more.

"Jozet, Lance called me and said that he thinks he's dying. He needs you to come to the hospital immediately."

"Are you sure you didn't misunderstand him? I was just there with him last night, and he looked like he was finally improving. Are you certain that's what he said?"

"I'm sure. He said the doctor had just been in and things looked pretty rough. I could hardly understand him, he was gasping so much." Mark hesitated a moment. "I'm worried, Jozet. He's feeling something. Something is really wrong this time. He's concerned about Jordan trying to handle this intense situation all by himself. I'm heading up there right now. I'll see you there."

The look in his eyes both convinced her the situation was serious, and gave her a boost of faith, as well. She knew Mark believed I would not die. Someway, somehow, God would deliver me. He always had.

But for the first time in many, many years she wondered if this might not be the end. As she drove to the hospital, her prayers were the most sincere and intense she had ever sent heavenward.

"If ever I needed an answer, dear Lord, I need to know now. Will he live? Or will he die this time? Is this the way it is to end?" The answer came back with a feeling of peace each time she asked. She only hoped that she was interpreting the message correctly.

Shortly after she arrived at the hospital, my mother and father came into my room. Doctors and nurses were briskly hanging bottles, changing medications, and moving me to a surgery cart. It had become an emergency now. The diagnosis was "respiratory failure". This required immediate surgical intervention or I would be dead.

The gurney was rushed down the hallway into the elevator. As the doors closed, a terrible silence set in. It now became a long game of waiting and wondering.

More and more family arrived to give support. They hugged

each other and tried to assure one another that all would be well, but the reality of the situation demanded serious contemplation. And what was supposed to have been one to two hours of surgery now began to drag on for what seemed forever. It would end up being four or five hours before it was concluded.

Dr. Michael Denyer, the chief surgeon, was very good to give updates during the long span. His report was direct, but compassionate. Things were not good. The right lung had two large abscesses in it, and it somehow had torn. Air was escaping through the tear. It had also become diseased with the ARDS (Adult Respiratory Distress Syndrome). The left lung was filled with blood clots and had become diseased, as well. Dr. Denyer tried to explain to my family what the ARDS disease was, and assure them everything that could possibly be done for me was being done in that surgical room.

There were friends who were part of the surgical team, and I know each gave special attention to saving my life. I will forever be thankful for the work they did that Sunday afternoon.

Jozet called her parents and told them the news. She said she had held up pretty well until that point. It was then, when she could confide her true fears and concerns to her parents, though, that she broke down and sobbed. She knew she had to be strong for the kids. They would never hear her say, "Dad is dying." She could not allow them to have anything but hope. But, privately, to her mother and father who knew her best, she had to share her innermost feelings.

As the hours passed and the family huddled together, many

prayers were sent heavenward. They knew my life was hanging by a very thin thread, and only God could intercede for me. What they could not know was that, with life support equipment keeping my body alive, my spirit had been set free for a time. I was truly in God's hands.

Around 6:00 p.m. the surgery was finally completed. I was wheeled to the Intensive Care Unit where my family was waiting. The doctors informed my family that, in an effort to try to save my life, they had to paralyze me and put me into a drug-induced coma. This would stop all bodily functions that were not absolutely necessary to survival. Those bodily functions that were essential were being assisted through life support equipment. A tracheotomy had been performed and I had been placed on a ventilator; a machine that would breath for me while I healed. Three chest tubes were inserted into the space between my chest wall and lungs which would allow the infectious fluid to drain. Sixteen different tubes and wires hung from my body carrying life sustaining medication, nourishment, and assistance that would enable me to survive. With these in place, my body could spend all the energy it still had, to heal. It was the best that could be done. Yet in all honesty, most of the medical personnel later confided in me, that they did not believe I would survive.

My family would now spend the next several weeks waiting and watching my body lying in a coma, not knowing whether I would live or die.

CHAPTER EIGHT

Learning By The Spirit

Entering into the Spirit World, or the dimension where spirits reside after this life, had taken place so quickly that I hardly discerned my location before seeing my dead relatives who were present to greet me. It was such a comforting aid to my arrival. Randy assured me that everyone who dies has close relatives and friends present to greet them when they pass through the veil which separates our two worlds.

I watched numerous people pass through that veil while I was there. It was most enjoyable. I witnessed an elderly woman whose family anticipated her arrival. They were jumping up and down excitedly, as if waiting for a loved one to come off an airplane. A slender man, who was most obviously the husband of the woman, paced back and forth nervously. Two women kept patting him on the back and excitedly hugging him as they anticipated the arrival. There was a group of nearly twenty individuals standing together.

Another man, who acted as a leader to the group, then stepped partly through the veil so that I could not see him. He then stepped back, announced happily, "It is time," and turned back into the veil. He reached his arm forward and drew it back holding the hand of the elderly woman. She seemed startled, and a bit blinded at first. Then upon seeing the group, her expression turned to one of absolute splendor. The group parted for her to see the gentleman standing at the back of the pack; the one who appeared to be her husband. They rushed into one another's arms. The entire company encircled them and eagerly welcomed her home.

I was deeply moved. I realized very quickly that a spirit can experience great extremes of emotion, as I was feeling at that moment.

"Is this how it happens?" I asked Randy, choked with emotion.

"Isn't it beautiful. I never tire of seeing it," he answered me.

The group began to walk away together. "They are going to where a family celebration has been planned," Randy explained.

"Celebration? I guess I had never thought of the Spirit World having celebrations. What is it like?"

"Oh, it's wonderful! Families get together when loved ones pass into our world. And they gather frequently to celebrate special events and occasions. For example the day of the Savior; the day of the birth of our Savior into mortality. All the heavens and the Spirit World rejoice exceedingly for that event! It is an incredible celebration," Randy continued.

"And they have a great feast," Uncle Howard, Randy's father who had died just a few short years ago, said as he stepped to Randy's side. He put his arm around Randy's shoulder and smiled at me.

"Eat?" I said. "You can eat in the Spirit World?" I could hardly believe he was serious.

"Randy seems to have gotten a good feel for it," Uncle Howard said laughingly.

Randy continued, "It wouldn't be heavenly without it!" He said triumphantly, as a man who knew whereof he spoke. "Oh, I wish you could stay to see it. It is most wonderful."

At that moment, two things he had said filled my mind. First, until that instant, I had not considered that this was not heaven. Though the abode was heavenly, it was a realm where spirits awaited their resurrections. Heaven was a place where God personally resided, a realm where resurrected beings could live.

"This is not Heaven, is it, Randy?" I sought to confirm.

"No, this is Paradise. It is a realm of absolute peace, a Zion, for those spirits who have lived righteous lives. You are right," he continued, having clearly discerned my thoughts, "God does not reside here. That is where Heaven is."

"Does he come here?" I asked.

"Oh, yes. He, as well as his angels who have assignments here, come to fulfill their work. I'll show you where they come."

Before we could leave, however, I had to ask my other question. "Randy, you said that you wished I could stay to see the great celebration for the birth of the Savior. Why couldn't I stay to see it? Is my feeling true? Am I going back to earth again?"

He smiled. "It's a little more complicated than that. There

are a few decisions that must be made by you, and by those who make those decisions here. I've been asked to be your escort. I've been assigned to take you to certain places and show you certain things. There is much we need to teach you. But I feel quite certain you will not be here very long. I'm confident the things you are to learn are for your help when you go back, not for here. You still have much to accomplish on earth. Be patient," he said, as he put his arm around the back of my neck and lovingly shook me. "You'll understand it better soon. Your memory has not come back much yet."

I was content, for the moment, with his answer. Something inside me seemed to tell me I had more to do on earth, but I could not quite grab hold of the source in my mind from whence these feelings came. It seemed as if my mind contained a memory bank, which, once opened, would help me remember important instructions and information. I recognized the propriety in Randy's advice; *be patient.*

It was also comforting to me to see Randy's demeanor. He had not changed much. Death had not dimmed his sense of humor. That was one thing I had always feared in death. The very word "death" seemed to signify "gloom", but I was finding out quickly I was gravely mistaken in my assumption. Humor is a good and wonderful part of our characters which God has instilled in us. And Randy had only improved his happy character, not changed it. Even his arm around my neck at that moment reminded me of his love for wrestling. Of a truth, death is not an end. It is but a transition in our pathway through eternity.

The other family members who had greeted me took their leave at this point. Each assured me I would see them again before I left. It seemed they were most certain of my return to earth. I asked Grandpa Mark why he was so certain I was going back, if there were decisions that yet had to be made.

"You're going back, my boy. You count on it. I know what you will choose, and I know what you have left to do." He gave me a quick hug and smiled. "You will be going back. You mark my words." I thanked him, hugged Grandma, and waved good-bye as they and the others headed away.

It was extremely interesting to me how each family member explained they were busy and needed to get back to their specific work and assignments, as they left. Each person, or spirit, was filled with love and peace, and each was anxiously involved in a work. I never did see an idle person the entire time I was in their world. Though there were many who were studying, numerous busily working, and others in happy discourse one with another, I never saw anyone who looked is if they had no idea of what to do. Theirs is a world of great order and direction.

As we began to walk away from my entrance place, I scanned the grayish curtain-like matter they had called the veil. It went on for as far as I could see. Throughout my experience I witnessed many individuals pass through it into the waiting arms of loved ones. It was not always at the same location as where I had entered. I concluded this was the reason for such varied, yet similar descriptions of the Spirit World from people who had shared near-death experiences. Some facts were so completely the same, such as the incredible peace each feels. But the surroundings were often different. Randy shared with me that their world is every bit as large as our world. In fact, it is in the same place, but a different dimension.

We began to walk down a pathway lined with varied flowers and foliage. I stopped to look closer at these beautiful plants. I kneeled and gently touched the petals and greenery. I felt a surge within me, as if these creations were seeking to say to my soul, "We, too, are creations of God. We have sought with diligence to create beauty and splendor of celestial magnitude. Have we done so? Have we filled your heart with joy in seeing us? Have we not fulfilled the measure of our creation?"

And I wanted to say back to them, "Oh, yes. Be at peace. You have given me great joy. Truly you have sought and fulfilled your purpose." Love was being radiated by them.

"How is it possible?" I thought. Then immediately the understanding came into my mind saying, "These are all my creations, as are you. They each have a spirit, as do you, yet theirs are different from those of mankind. They are completely content as plant life, as are my animals. The purpose of their creation is different from your creation. And as they fulfill that measure of their creation, they receive a fullness of joy. There is order in all things of my kingdom."

The words were truth, and love filled me. All plants and animals are God's creations and He loves them. And I gained a much greater respect and love for them at that moment.

But there was more. More teaching was occurring inside me.

I realized that the truth of the words conveyed to me had brought an additional level of peace and warmth to my soul. I knew it was truth, for I could feel it was so. Truth can be discerned by its feeling. When we hear or are given truth, it brings a burst of warmth and additional strength of what they call Spirit. It is light to our souls. And it matters not whether this truth conveyed is concerning spiritual laws of repentance or the laws of physics used in the creative process. Each is truth. And truth is always witnessed within us by the illuminating light and warmth of this spirit.

A voice within me helped me understand that this principle was a truth which I could carry with me to discern the light from the darkness in our world, as well. If it is truth, the Spirit will be there.

"Thereby, you may know what is truth. And the truth shall set you free," the voice of the Spirit taught me.

I was consumed in this spirit. I burned with a warmth of love and illuminating light. I looked at Randy as he knelt beside me. He knew what I had experienced. I saw it filling him, too, as he looked into my eyes.

"You feel it, too, don't you Randy."

"Yes, Lance," he said, with a look of complete understanding. "You are being taught by the Holy Spirit. It is the Spirit of God which illuminates all truth and light. It is light. And that Spirit can teach you all things." He waited for a moment, knowing what I was feeling. Then he continued. "What you are experiencing is the truest form of learning."

All I could do was sit for a moment and bask in the magnitude of what I was feeling. I was completely overcome. I had never known such a thirst for knowledge. It seemed unquenchable! …As if I were a cup that could never be filled, wanting more and more. I wanted to never to be left alone, away from that light and truth which filled me at that moment. There was a yearning to learn and progress forever.

Somehow the greatness and omnipotence of our God seemed more understandable at that moment. Truly, He possesses a fullness of that unquenchable fire. For all truth is of Him.

Words are so weak. The exhilaration I felt must be one of those unspeakable things of the Spirit, for I am completely incapable of describing it adequately. It must be learned and felt by oneself. Yet I must share with you, I felt a thirst for knowledge such as I have never known. And it was filled with love and light. Perhaps, the love of God is far more encompassing than we have ever understood.

CHAPTER NINE

Music and Temples

When I had regained my composure after my lesson of learning by the Spirit, I stood and thanked Randy for his patience with me.

"Certainly, Lance," Randy said. "I understand. Remember, I, too, had these experiences after my arrival. My hope is that I can give you a chance to taste of some of the exciting things you have in store. That is, once you are here for good."

From that time on, we talked as if things were not permanent. However, later, after several weeks had transpired with me still in my coma, I began to worry I would not make it back. It just seemed that I had been away too long, and it really started worrying me.

I was given the chance to go to my hospital room and see my body lying there. It looked so awful. I knew it would take a major miracle from God to make my body functional again. And, thankfully, He did grant one.

"Lance, look at the sky," Randy said, pointing heavenward. It was fantastic! The sky was a beautiful hue of deep blue straight above us, and showed gorgeous strands of violets, reds, oranges, and yellows along the horizon. It was as if there was a majestic sunset.

Looking upward I could see other planets in their orbits. They were so much easier to see than from our world. I could see planets of various size. They appeared to be much closer. The Spirit taught me through my thoughts at that moment, that this was due to the heightened abilities of my senses as a spirit, rather than the planets actually being so much closer. I never learned what planets I had seen, but the view was spectacular.

Randy shared with me that he had received opportunities to do some exploring throughout some of these other creations of God while he had been in the Spirit World. It didn't surprise me. He had loved hiking and exploring in the mountains as a young man. I would have loved to have had more time at that moment to discuss what he had experienced. But there were others waiting for us, he explained.

"Come with me, Lance." Randy took me by the hand and we headed down a white stone pathway. As we hurried toward our destination I was trying to soak in all of the new surroundings. There were many people in view. Each seemed so full of peace and happiness. I could not imagine someone not being completely content and joyous in this sphere. It would be impossible.

Suddenly I looked directly in front of us. We were approaching the most magnificent, glowing, white building I had ever seen. It appeared to be made of white marble and granite. It shot upward for nearly 100 feet, then stepped inward for, perhaps, twenty feet. It continued to stair step in this manner toward the heavens until I could see no higher.

There was a massive upper courtyard paved in gold which encircled the entire building. Then, from the front where we were now standing, approximately fifty stairs of gold descended to a lower courtyard lying in front of two enormous doors. These doors, also, appeared to be of solid gold. The entire structure seemed awesome in its size and structure.

"Wow!" was all I could manage to say. "That is magnificent!"

Randy chuckled. "It's pretty impressive, isn't it. This is a temple," Randy explained.

"A temple? I thought temples were for our world. Why would you have a temple here?" I asked.

"There is sacred work that must be done here, which is different from that performed on earth. These temples also serve as portals to Heaven."

"What do you mean?" I said.

"Remember, Lance, this is not Heaven. Heaven is where God resides. When those who live in Heaven need to pass into the Spirit World to do their work, they do so through these temples," he explained. "The Spirit World is composed of two areas; Paradise, which is where we are and is the abode for those who lived righteous lives, and Spirit Prison, where those who sought evil in their lives reside."

Randy shared with me some of the important meetings that occur in these temples, and the sacredness of their functions. Once again I felt the rushing and warmth of the Spirit testifying to me what he spoke was truth.

We were now standing in the upper courtyard of the temple. I looked behind me, as people were busily passing by us. There were several long keyboards which appeared to be suspended in air about waist high. They were encased in this same white marble type substance. There were black and white keys, as a piano in our world, yet the keyboard seemed to extend further in each direction with additional keys. There were many individuals working on them. There was no confusion of noise, however. It seemed you could tune into each board as you desired. I had not even heard the music until I sought to understand their purpose.

A young woman, dressed in an elegant white robe, with beautiful blonde hair tumbling down her back turned and looked to me.

"Hi. I am Beverly," she said with a smile. "Would you like to try something?"

"I'm afraid I might ruin the peace in Paradise if I were to play," I confessed. She laughed.

"That is not important. We are using music to learn important eternal truths. Music is a most powerful conductor of the Spirit. We use music to help us in our learning process," she explained.

"All music?" I asked.

"Well, let's say all true music. In your world you have much that could never be conducive to the Holy Spirit." She paused a minute. Then continued, "I'm sure you have experienced it. Haven't you listened to selections of music and have been moved to tears? Quite often, when you are moved to tears, it is because the Spirit is intensely present. Do you understand?"

"I do," I said. I smiled at her, then scanned the great number of spirits using these keyboards. Many had papers they were studying in connection with what they were playing.

"Do you want to try it?" Beverly asked.

"I guess. You're sure I won't destroy Paradise?" She laughed and nodded that it would be OK. I was impressed with the incredible happiness she spread with her smile and pleasant nature. It made me wish to be more like her. She and Randy carried such a peace. It was very contagious.

There are parts of my experience which are hazy and, for one reason or another, I cannot remember them. Unfortunately, my experience of using the keyboard and the further learning of eternal truths is one of them. I cannot remember what took place next, but I was left with a most certain validation that music is a great tool of God. Great truths may be learned by using uplifting music as a conductor of the Spirit. I have always enjoyed music, but I gained a much deeper respect for its eternal purpose.

I do remember as we concluded our meeting with Beverly, we hugged. Then I thanked her for the astounding truths which she had shared with me.

I will forever remember her, for our lives touched one another. Not only by the lessons of music, but by what takes place when Spirits embrace. Some of the grandest experiences of my visit were my opportunities to exchange greetings with others. For, in their world, they do not wave "hello" or shake hands; they hug. A Spirit can feel another Spirit just as we can feel flesh to flesh. And so they embrace one another. And when they embrace, an amazing experience occurs. It is as if your spirits transfer a feeling and synopsis of your life to one another. Suddenly you know and understand a person in ways far beyond any verbal communication. It creates an instant bond one to another; a friendship to build a foundation for loving one another more perfectly. Oh, how I missed those hugs when I left.

CHAPTER TEN

While I Was Sleeping

I do not know how long I was actually in the Spirit World. It is impossible to know the answer. It was very clear, time is of a different nature in their world than it is in ours. It would take a lengthy period of time to share all that I saw, heard, and experienced while I was gone. Perhaps I was only absent for five minutes at a time. Yet, maybe it lasted weeks, as it seemed. I really don't know.

I said "absent for five minutes at a time," for I remember coming and going at least three times. I was actually sent back into my body on three occasions. That was, perhaps, the most difficult part of my entire experience.

Randy and I had visited numerous locations in their world when word was delivered by a female messenger that I was to go back. She was most caring and friendly, and made it clear my departure was not for good. I was coming back to the Spirit World soon.

The messenger, Randy, and I were transported to the veil, at an astonishing speed. "It felt as if we were sucked through space to the location of my entrance through the veil. Suddenly we were standing there. I was given some instructions, told by Randy that he would meet me when I was to leave my body again, and cautioned as to the extreme pain that I would feel when I re-entered my body.

"Your mortal body is experiencing serious pain at this moment. Yet even that pain will not be as severe as the pain which is felt upon re-entry into one's body. You will feel excruciating pain for a moment, then a rush of the incredible pain your body is now enduring," the messenger informed me.

"Will I be awake or will I be unconscious when I return to my body?" I asked, as I began to feel some definite trepidation.

"Your body is presently in a coma, Lance. But you will feel some of the pain, and you will hear the voices of those around you, though you probably will not have any ability to respond. They have given your body heavy medications in an effort to help it relax and heal," the messenger continued. "I am so sorry that you must endure this. But I have been told it is necessary."

I could see by the look in her eyes she felt great compassion for my plight. And yet, as terrible as it sounded, I felt no urge to petition for reconsideration by whomever made such decisions. I had a peace inside that what had to be, must be.

I embraced Randy, then stepped through the veil. I was immediately drawn into my body. The pain was intense, as they had warned. Fortunately, it did not last long. But then I became aware of the fact that I was in my body, and began to feel the pain it was enduring.

It was a most unusual feeling. I felt as if I were in a series of dreams, and in the dreams I was suffocating. These dreams would continue on and on. I could understand why the doctors had paralyzed me, for I would have sought to fight and struggle had I been able to do so. It was like a never ending nightmare.

I am not certain how long I was back inside my body. I believe it was for days at a time, but cannot be certain.

I do remember hearing voices at times, as if I were in a deep hole and could hear the voices above me, but was too far away to be able to respond.

My family tells me there were times when I clearly showed signs of life, and other times when I really appeared to be dead. Perhaps both of these observations were accurate.

My wife tells me of a day when they allowed my older sons to come into my room to see me. A very serious strain of staph infection called MRSA had infiltrated my system, and medications were not killing it. Because of that, anyone coming into my room had to wear protective gowns, masks, and gloves.

My seven year old son, Jared, took his turn to come into the room and see me. Jozet told him to talk to me, as the doctors had told my family that by speaking to me continually, it would help keep my mind active so it wouldn't shut down completely. This would help in the rehabilitation process once I was awake, they explained. So Jared began to talk to me.

Jozet said that Jared walked to my side and said, "Dad, are you in there?" He then took his finger and lifted up each eye lid and looked into my eyes. They were rolled back so that only the whites showed.

Jared turned to my wife and said, "He isn't in there, Mom."

She looked at my face and saw the absolute appearance of one who was dead.

"I think you are right, buddy. Maybe he is visiting Jesus right now."

Jared's eyes lit up. "Yeah! I bet that's where he is."

"I'm sure he will be back soon," she concluded. She tried to smile reassuringly over the feelings of panic that were rising within her heart.

On another occasion my father said that he had come to visit me on a weekend, a few weeks after I had entered into the coma. My father is a state senator, and the Senate was in session while I was in the coma. Dad would fly to Boise each Sunday evening, take care of his business and attend sessions during the week, then fly back Friday evening to Idaho Falls. Mom would pick him up and they would drive to the hospital to see how I was doing. My mother also updated him daily over the phone.

On this particular visit he tried to speak to me to see if he could get any kind of response. He had done so at other times and had found no reaction, but this time it was different.

"Lance, it's Dad. How are you doing, pal? If you can hear me try to respond." He thought for a moment. "Lance, if you hear me, raise your eye brows."

He watched for a minute, then slowly I began raising my eyebrows. He and Mom were ecstatic! They cheered and asked me to do it again. I did it again. It gave them great hope that I would someday be back with them. It was one of the few times I showed real signs of being alive.

While I was in the comatose state, numerous other problems had developed in my system. The medical records show that my pancreas began to have serious problems, as well as the kidneys and gall bladder. I became diabetic for a period of time. The abscesses in the collapsed right lung continued to drain infection and fluid. The damage in the lungs and the seriousness of the staph infection, which had set in, were increasing. The list of diagnoses included 27 medical problems they had to confront. Without a doubt, things were not getting better, they were getting worse.

A team of doctors were working on my case, with experts in many different fields. Each, a highly respected physician who worked tirelessly to find answers.

My father's cousin, Dr. Newell Richardson, is a radiologist. He came to assist my family through the ordeal. Serious decisions had to be made, and it was comforting to my family to have another family member be able to look at the films, talk with the doctors, and understand exactly where things stood. On several occasions, my doctors, wife and parents huddled together and discussed possible options to save my life.

Approximately three weeks into the coma, it was decided there was nothing else that could be done for me at that particular hospital. There was one more procedure that could possibly be tried at the University of Utah hospital in Salt Lake City. But that would require a life flight which they were not certain I could survive. It was, also, a long shot as to whether the technique, which was experimental, could even save me. But they were down to final options, and it was their last hope for my survival. One of the doctors contacted the University of Utah Medical Center and explained my case. They agreed to accept me, but there were no beds currently available.

Meanwhile hundreds of prayers were being sent heavenward on my behalf. My immediate family, friends, and relatives throughout the country had been notified, and each was petitioning heaven. It is interesting to note that, during that same period, some of the dead relatives of those who were praying for me here, were those comforting and teaching me in the Spirit World.

My brother, Mark, my father and I had done a radio talk show each weekday morning for several years. With Dad in session in the Senate, Mark was carrying the show on his own. He shared with the listening audience some details concerning my accident and condition. Many of these faithful friends also began to pray on my behalf. With so many family and friends on each side of the veil pulling for me, Heaven surely listened.

Meanwhile it was becoming more and more difficult for my family to cope with the situation. Day after day the reports were showing my condition worsening. With weeks having passed, my children began to worry whether their father would ever be with them again. Jozet would join the kids together for prayer every chance she could get. She spoke only positively to the children about my recovery. She knew they needed that hope.

My mother and my wife took long turns sitting with me, as well as some other family members. With Jozet trying to keep some semblance of normality for the kids, Mom volunteered to be with me more of the time. The days became long, the nights even longer. Mom wore herself out watching and caring for me.

My sons would take any opportunity the hospital staff would allow to come visit me. On one occasion Jared received another turn to visit. He had seen no response from me at any time he had visited.

"Dad, do you want me to tell you about what is happening in pro football?" Jared asked, knowing football was a common love we shared. Then he shared the news he had heard concerning the playoffs and Super Bowl.

"I will tell you about how I am doing in school now." Jared took my hand and massaged it as he spoke. He wanted desperately to see a reaction, some movement or sign that I knew he was there. And more than anything, that I was yet alive and would one day walk with him out the door of the hospital. But there was nothing.

Someone came into the room and informed Jared it was time for him to go. Jozet sat nearby and watched her son holding my hand.

"Dad, they said that I have to go now." He looked at my face, as emotions swelled within him.

"Dad, I love you. And I am not going to let anything take you away. I promise! I don't care what happens, I'll keep you. OK, Dad?" Tears were now flowing freely down his face, as they were his mother's.

And then something wonderful happened. A large single tear trickled down the side of my face. It was much too large to be sweat or moisture. He knew that somehow his father had heard him, and ached to respond.

"Dad, we saw that! You cried, you cried!" he shouted. "You really are there!" Then he paused a moment again, knowing his time was gone.

"Oh, Dad. I love you so much. Please come back to me."

Though I could not move or speak, I heard him that day. I was there. And I would have given anything at that moment to hold my son and promise him I would return. Oh, thank God, for allowing that tear to fall.

CHAPTER ELEVEN

Principles of
A Zion Society

I can't tell you what a relief it was to leave my body and return to the Spirit World. This occurred, to my recollection, twice after the initial visit.

I remember feeling a sudden swooshing feeling as I was taken, once again, out of my body. This time, instead of seeing only darkness, I saw my body lying in the hospital bed. I saw the room and equipment. None of my family were in the room with me at that moment. But Randy was standing there waiting to escort me back into the Spirit World. I appreciated so much his companionship through all of this. My closeness to him helped give me a stability and comfort as I explored and experienced what, for me, were uncharted territories.

"Hi, Lance. It's time to go back," Randy said with an outstretched hand. "Are you ready?"

I gratefully took his hand and followed him through the veil back into their world of Paradise.

The relief from the pain was so immediate and wonderful. I sometimes wonder if I could have lived had I had to endure the entire comatose state in my body. The pain was so excruciating. I was very appreciative of the rest I received during the periods of time I was taken to the Spirit World, regardless of how long that time actually was.

Randy smiled at me and asked, "Are you glad to be back?"

"Oh, yes. But I know for certain, now, that I want to go back to mortality. I want to live again. I heard the voices of my family while I was there. My family still needs me. I think it's the right thing," I answered.

Randy smiled again. "You never know how much your family means to you until you are gone from them, do you." I nodded in agreement.

"I remember when I left to come here," Randy continued. "I had suffered so long that it was a welcomed rest to leave my bodily pain, but, oh how I missed my family at first. I wondered if it was right for me to have died. But then I was shown what is about to happen in your world. And it was explained to me that certain members of each family chose, long ago, before this life, to die and come to this realm that they might better help their families endure what is about to happen."

Randy's expression changed to one of reverence. "There are many powerful, wonderful spirits who are being called home right now, that they can better help their families prepare for that which is about to take place in your world. One of the major reasons many of us are here is to serve and help those in mortality. Remember that word "serve" for it is a vital part of our world, and can change yours." His eyes did not move from mine. I knew what he was saying was deeply important.

"Lance, do you understand what I am saying to you? I have

helped you many times in your life. I have been given assign-ments on several occasions to assist you and inspire you."

Randy then shared several stories of times when he had helped me. Each was a time I could remember, and I became deeply thankful to God, to know He had sent someone whom I loved so much to help in those times when I had needed help so desperately. And again I gained a greater appreciation for fami-ly and its eternal function.

Uncle Howard had approached as we were talking. He had listened to Randy explain what he had done to help me.

"I, too, have similar assignments," he explained. "There is other work I must do, as well, but I am often called upon to help my wife and children who are yet in mortality."

He then shared with me experiences he'd had with his wife and each of his children. "Tell them of these things, will you? I want them to know that I love them dearly, and am often sent by the Lord to assist them."

I was deeply moved. I had never understood nor thought of how God delivers assistance to us. With billions of children, what more perfect plan could he use than through righteous family members? It made me think about how often I may have been given inspiration from God through ministering "family" servants of God. I could believe it was truth. And once again I felt that burning warmth inside, testifying to me that it was.

We walked as we talked and passed into an area that remind-ed me of a town plaza. It was a large open area with a white, marble-looking floor. Many spirits were quickly passing back and forth across this area into sections of buildings lined upon streets. Without asking, it was made known to my mind that these buildings were places where the work of the Spirit World was done, where meetings took place between those who had particular assignments.

This was also where the functions of their society took place. They were not busy establishing themselves or furthering themselves for financial or selfish reasons. No, rather they recognized that all that they had received, came as a gift from our Father in Heaven, and so they shared it with each other completely. Their sincere desires were for the good and betterment of the whole. Each took particular interest in the welfare and happiness of those around them. Their "inner peace" came from the love they exhibited for their brothers and sisters of the entire heavenly family.

Family means those to whom you are physically related. But it also has a greater circumference which encompasses all of God's children. And they love one another without regard for race, creed, or religion as so many of us do in our world.

As the truths, which make their society such a Zion or Paradise, were being distilled upon my soul, I could only look around and bask in the perfection of it all. I wanted to bottle these principles and feelings and carry it back with me.

About that time Randy turned to me and announced, "Lance, there are some friends of yours who have come to see you."

With that, I turned and watched two men dressed in white robes approaching, who instantly were known to my spirit. I felt a flood of emotions erupt within me. I cried as I wrapped my arms around them and welcomed them. These were two of my best friends. But not from this mortal life. I had known them when all of us lived as spirits with God, before we were born into mortality. My spirit, however remembered them completely. I loved them now as I did then.

One of them had lived nearly two hundred years ago, and the other had lived on the earth thousands of years before I had. But this did not matter. I yet knew and loved them from our association in heaven before we were born.

"It is so good to see you," I said. "How have you been?"

Ben, who stood a bit over six feet tall and carried a powerful build, spoke first. "We are very good. We were both so excited to hear you had been allowed to visit this world. We have been informed you will be going back soon, but we were asked to visit you and help you remember some important matters."

Samuel, who had lived long ago, also stood nearly six feet tall. His build was smaller than Ben's, but was still strong. He had very striking good looks, with black wavy hair. He spoke to me with an easy smile.

"Lance, the Lord knows and loves you. He truly knows each of us and is our Savior. Can you remember that?"

I felt deep inside me, attempting to remember our life before we were born. Short segments of that existence came into my mind. "I can remember just a little," I informed them.

"That's fine. Your memory has not completely come back yet. Over time you will continue to remember more and more.

Were you to remain here, you would regain all that you previously knew," Samuel continued. "Jesus Christ, your older brother and Savior, wants you to remember His love for you. He loves each of us with a most perfect love. For that reason He *did* suffer and die for us."

As they spoke, my mind began to open as if a screen were before me. I suddenly remembered how each of us loved Him. We adored and worshiped Him. Only through Him was our salvation. Yes, I knew Him and loved Him.

With that memory in place, a larger part of my mind had been opened. I remembered that each of us had promised our Lord we would do certain things with our lives. There were reasons why we were born when we were born, and it mattered. Ben and Samuel helped me remember some of the things I had promised to do with my life. I was not yet done. I had not accomplished all I was to do.

I suddenly felt an incredible desire to get back to earth. I wanted so badly to finish my work. I knew I could never be happy staying in their world, regardless of its wonder and peace, unless I finished my work. Not that my work was any more special than that of anyone else. No, what mattered was that I did not want to let down my Lord and God. I had to return and fulfill my assignments. I could not be at peace knowing I had not finished.

"I remember! I now understand why you were sent. Your presence has helped me remember the promises I made long ago to God. I cannot stay here. I must go back," I concluded.

Ben and Samuel smiled and embraced me. "That is right, Lance," Ben said. "You have remembered. We love you and would most enjoy having you here, but we know what you must do, and the Lord will be pleased with your decision. Ultimately, Lance, it is yours to decide. God has given you that agency to choose. It is your choice. But we are very pleased with your decision."

"You should know, though, Lance, there are some difficult days ahead in your world. The prophecies from the scriptures are about to unfold," Samuel warned. "There will be times when you will wish you were back here again. But do not steady your eye upon this. You must, instead, keep your eye upon the greatness of the Zion which is soon to be built in your world."

I knew of the scriptures concerning Zion. I had researched the ancient Zion, the biblical city of Enoch, for several years in an effort to understand how those people had attained a perfect and total peace. I had co-authored a book about the people of Enoch's city and what took place in their efforts to create such a society. We had researched through the Dead Sea scrolls, Nag Hamadi scrolls, three scrolls of Enoch that have been found, as well as interviewed numerous cultures around the world who have information in their histories concerning the ancient city of Enoch. Our hope was that by studying their society we could find some of the answers for the problems we face today. It appeared that this was true. All that I had seen of this Zion, or Paradise, in the Spirit World confirmed it. I was learning that there are principles of a Zion society which, if learned and lived, will bring the same peace and love I was then feeling. And that peace was so incredible I felt that I would do anything to keep it.

With all that I had researched and learned concerning such societies, I was overjoyed to be given such an amazing opportunity to see and be taught concerning the principles which create a Zion.

"You are so lucky!" Samuel exclaimed. "Do you see? You are the ones who will build the New Jerusalem spoken of by all the prophets since the beginning of time; the Zion of the last days. It is to come in your day. Every prophet since the beginning of time has yearned to see and be a part of this. It will be a day when a paradise will be created on earth. It will be built in your country of America. And the peaceful ones of the earth shall come unto it. Do you understand what an incredible day that shall be? The very God of Heaven and Earth shall come down to it, for it will be as a heaven on earth. Yes, there are some dark days to come before it arrives, but the blessings and glory of that day far outshine the trials which you must endure first. Re-read the scriptures, for they tell you all these things, and it is soon time for them to take place."

I was filled with excitement by his words. To think that we might have an opportunity to see that day, and, perhaps, even live in that city. I could not hope for anything greater. And God will come unto it? Truly this would be Paradise.

I looked at Ben, Samuel, Randy, and Uncle Howard. I could feel their excitement and I had a greater understanding of their meaning far beyond the words, for they spoke spirit to spirit.

Thus, I had felt their emotions, seen their vision, and experienced their message.

"Lance, this is the destiny of America, if the people choose *Liberty*. This was the vision of the founding fathers when they sought to form such a Union," Ben explained. He had lived in America in its early days and had seen the possibility of its future.

"Some of those founding fathers were given vision and understanding from God concerning the fact that they were laying a foundation for the Zion of the last days to be built. The Constitution would help safeguard a freedom where it could begin and grow. They were not perfect men, but they were some of the best God had. And their efforts were greatly inspired."

Samuel put his hand on my shoulder. "Lance, there are some others who are waiting to meet with you and share more with you concerning this. We will go to them shortly." He looked into my eyes and gave me a look of friendship and love that I hope I will never forget. He seemed to have an ever present smile, but now it was filled with even deeper meaning.

"Oh, Lance, we love you. We have watched your life and have been eager to see you. You are a dear brother and friend. But we know you have come to realize your family still needs you, too. Enjoy each day with them. They pass so quickly. Before you know it, you will be embracing each son and your daughter and sending them on their own. These feelings last beyond the grave, my brother. Love is eternal, and so is the family. Both your own, and God's family."

I felt an incredible yearning to go back to see my family, and to fulfill the promises I had made to God long ago. And I had a passion inside to one day see such a paradise on earth; one such as the one I was then experiencing.

"Would you like to see your family?" Randy asked. "Oh, yes. I would love to see them. Can I?"

"You can. Come with me and I will give you a chance to see them," he replied.

I turned and embraced Uncle Howard and my friends. They told me they would meet me shortly. But for now, I was going to go visit my family. No news could have sounded sweeter.

CHAPTER TWELVE

Soon,
I'll Be Back

I took Randy's hand and followed him into the veil. This time, however, we were not going to my hospital room. We were going to where my wife and children were at that moment.

"Your children are in school. Do you want to go see them in their classrooms?" Randy asked.

"Sure! It seems like forever since I last saw them," I said. I could hardly wait to see them.

It felt as if we were flying through space and time as we headed to the schools. Then, almost instantly we had arrived at the grade school of three of my boys. I found myself standing in my son Creed's classroom.

I looked at him and smiled. It was a relief to see life had continued on. It was greater relief to see my son was happy and healthy. He was deeply engrossed in something his teacher was reading to the class. I watched him race to get his hand in the air first in answer to a question. He won, and answered the question correctly. I chuckled to myself. It was so interesting to be standing there next to my son and no one had any idea I was there.

I looked at Randy standing at the back of the class and smiled. "This is really amazing! They don't have any idea we are here, do they?" Randy nodded with agreement.

We passed into each of my other son's classrooms and watched as they studied and talked to others in the classroom. The last one we visited was my oldest son, Brock.

Brock was in the junior high. He had his head turned with his chin positioned in his hand, elbow on his desk. I could hear his thoughts at that moment. I believe the only reason I was able to hear his thoughts was because he was thinking about me right then. He was thinking about what I must be doing and how I was feeling like at that time.

I heard him say in his mind, "I wonder how Dad is doing today? I wonder if he's in terrible pain?" He paused a moment, then thought, "Maybe he isn't even there! Maybe God has allowed him to leave his body and go into Heaven while his body gets better. Oh! That would be so cool!"

"Brock, I'm coming back, buddy. I *am* coming back," I said, trying desperately to let him hear me and know I was fine. "They've promised me I'm coming back. I'll see you soon, son. I love you."

It was time for us to leave. I watched Brock lie his head down on his desk and put his arm at an angle around the top of his head on the front of the desk. He looked good, and it was nice to see he was thinking of me.

Randy escorted me to where my wife was, and then, told me he would be back in a minute. My wife was driving our '94 Suburban into town at the time. I was able to literally sit down in the passenger seat next to her. The radio was on and she was singing along with it. It happened to be a song called, "God must have spent a little more time on you." She was crying as she sang along. There was no doubt of whom she was thinking at that moment.

I watched her momentarily and kind of chuckled to think I was sitting there watching her singing. But the song and her tears touched me deeply. As she wiped tears from her cheeks, I began to feel emotional, as well. I began to cry.

"Jozet, dear. I love you. I am coming back. They have promised me now that I get to come back." I watched for any reaction from her that might tell me she was feeling my presence or hearing my words in her mind.

"I am really coming back, dear, I really am. Just hold on a while longer." Then she turned and looked my direction. I could not tell at that moment if she knew I was there, but she seemed as if she had felt something.

I watched her look around her, as if to see if someone was there.

"Honey, I'm here. I'm right here by your side. I will be back soon, and then I will never leave your side."

Jozet later shared with me that she remembered that ride very well, and indeed had looked to see if someone was there. She had felt something, and had told our children when she arrived home that day, "Dad was with me in the car today. I know it. I felt him next to me. But somehow I know he is not dead; he is coming back. I felt that thought come to my mind, and I know it's true."

Yes, God was 'spending a little more time on me'.

THE MESSAGE

CHAPTER THIRTEEN

It's Really All True, Isn't It

Randy escorted me back into the Spirit World after I had adequate time to see my family and know they were safe and taken care of. It was a most meaningful experience for me. One night after I had recovered and left the hospital, I shared with my family the experience of going to see each of them. I told each son what I had seen them doing. With eyes wide and chins dropped, one by one they remembered the very things that I told them I had seen. They knew it was true, and they knew I had been there.

As Randy and I passed back by the plaza area in the Spirit World, I once again saw hundreds of people busily heading to their different locations. As we began to cross the plaza on our way to meet with Ben, Samuel, and those whom they said were waiting for me, we met several other relatives and friends of mine. It appeared that they had been notified I was present and they wanted to see me and have me pass on greetings to their family members in the mortal world.

I saw my Great Grandma and Grandpa Nelson with some of our other relatives. We embraced, and spent some time talking about different family members. Grandma shared with me that she had recently been helping my younger sister, Kristi, through a difficult divorce and the trials of being a single mother.

"Oh, how I love that girl," Grandma said. "She is so special to me." I had not known she had felt so close to Kristi. But I was once again moved with great gratitude to God for sending help in a time of considerable need.

As we parted company I hadn't taken more than two or three steps when my Great Uncle Ken greeted me. He is my Grandpa Sam Gordon's brother, and I had known him well before his death. He looked so good. He, (as were most of the spirits I met in my experience there), was dressed in white. It was a white jump suit. He looked much younger than when I had last seen him before his death. He talked with me concerning my grandfather and of what a wonderful man he is. I shared my gratitude with him for his loving personality and told him how much I appreciated and loved my Grandpa. We embraced and continued on our way.

Randy led me past the buildings of white and down a pathway leading into a meadow. It was most beautiful, bordered on the left by an impressive mountain range. The towering peaks boasted splendid jagged crags and massive cliffs. A gorgeous waterfall descended from thousands of feet on high to a quiet pool below. The pool rested in a serene meadow flanked by green foliage, which progressed into a variety of colors in the bushes and trees. A mighty golden eagle soared above us. The peace was so enthralling that no one would ever want to leave.

As I looked upon the beauty, my eyes were suddenly caught by a mighty lion breaking through the bushes into the meadow.

He looked directly at me. My immediate reaction was one of fear and I tensed. I looked at Randy. He chuckled, then turned to look at the lion.

The lion began to walk right towards me until he stood exactly by my left side. Suddenly, it was as if I heard the lion's spirit communicating to me, in my mind.

"It's all right. Don't be afraid. All God's creations are safe in this kingdom." I felt a love being radiated from this mighty beast.

Randy turned to me and said, "Go ahead. Pet him." The animal leaned its head to the back of my hand and rubbed its mane against it. I slowly raised my hand and began to stroke his long coarse hair. It was interesting to me that, although we were both spirits, I could still feel the hair. I believe all things must have been created spiritually first, then temporally. The spirit retains those characteristics.

As I petted this great king I felt a desire to radiate love back to him and let him know that I loved him, as well. It was returned to me again.

Suddenly I looked up and saw a mother deer walking across the meadow not more than twenty feet behind the lion. She had a fawn at her side. They calmly looked at the lion; the lion looked at them. There was nothing but peace between them.

"Not in our world," I immediately thought. "In our world this would never be seen." Truly the lamb and lion shall lie together in Paradise. And so it shall be, as the scriptures tell us, in the days of that Millennial Zion of the last days.

I was impressed by the instant feeling of love I felt for all animal life. I knew of a certainty that God loves these creatures. It is important that we show respect for them.

As another lesson had been deeply implanted in my mind, we took our leave and continued down the stone pathway stretching into the distance.

As we traveled on our way to meet with Ben, Samuel, and others, we came upon two separate friends of mine who had died almost exactly one year before. They had been notified I was there and had come to say hello. It was wonderful to see each of them. Both looked so good. One had died of cancer, while the other had been caught in an avalanche while snowmobiling. It had been difficult for their families and friends to lose them. So, it was particularly good to see them again.

We embraced, and I felt their love radiating to me. My friend who had died of cancer then had to leave.

I asked my friend, whom we will call Rick, how he was doing.

"I absolutely love it here!" Rick began. "But my wife's pain is hurting me." I knew she had been having a very difficult time coping with his loss. They are the parents of five children, which made it all the more difficult for her to handle all of this alone. "Lance, you need to go talk to her and let her know that it was right that I died. I know that now." He then shared how it had been difficult for him to accept when he first found that he was dead.

"But after they escorted me into this world and showed me the plan for me and my family, I then knew it was right."

We talked of his family, especially of his children, and how he is able to help them in ways he could not have from our world. The work with his family was a very important reason for why he had died when he did.

Rick was a large, rough, and tough man in mortality. We had wrestled one another when we were in high school, and had remained friends ever since. He was a fun-loving individual and had been extremely close to his children. Rick worked hard and played hard, and enjoyed his time with his family. His sister had dated my cousin Randy for a period of time just before Randy had died of leukemia. In fact, both Rick's sister and Randy had leukemia at the same time. But she had recovered and lived.

I knew Rick had always believed in God and had been pretty religious in his life. But I believe he had, as all of us do at times, wondered if God really existed; had Christ really suffered, died, and been resurrected; was He the Son of God and our Savior, and was there really life after death.

But now he was a teacher of these truths. In my time in their world I met people who had belonged to a variety of different religions. But no one remotely questioned whether or not Jesus Christ was the God of our world, the very Son of God, our Redeemer and Savior. This is common knowledge that we remember, once we go to the Spirit World, concerning our life with God before we were born into mortality. Rick now taught Christ's gospel of salvation to those who had not known His plan in their lives. A great many had died without this knowledge and he was being given the opportunity to teach these truths.

He loved it, as well as his work with his family. My other friend was likewise involved in such work.

"Lance, we are needing to go now," Randy informed us. "I am sorry to cut this short, but there are those who are awaiting us."

"Rick, it has been so good to see you," I said as I embraced him to leave. Rick pulled back and looked long and hard into my eyes. Then he said something that I hope I will never forget, nor the feeling at that moment.

"Lance, it's really true, isn't it. It is really all true." The Spirit rushed within me, and once again I felt that feeling of warmth and light testifying to me that his words were of truth. I *knew* it, too. Yes, without any doubt, God lives and is the Father of us all. Yes, there is, indeed, life after death, for I had seen and experienced it. And yes, we could be redeemed through the atoning blood of Jesus Christ, our Lord and Savior. I smiled and looked deep inside his eyes, knowing whereof he spoke.

"Yes, it's true. It is really all true."

Rick grabbed me by both shoulders, then raising one finger and pointing it at me, said, "You tell my family I am going to make darn sure we are together forever, no matter what it takes."

I promised him I would deliver his message and we left.

Though time has passed since my experience, I can never forget Rick's final message, for it epitomized more than any other statement made to me, the importance of what I learned while in their world. It is true. It is really all true.

CHAPTER FOURTEEN

Liberty

It was time. We were to meet with a group of men who had a most important message for me. Grandpa Mark joined us as we passed down the walkway. He smiled and patted me on the back and talked to us as we continued on our way.

I knew we could have traveled quicker had they wanted to, but they desired a chance for me to see some more of the beauties of their world, the buildings, and the people. Everything was in such perfect order. I wished our world could be as theirs, then remembered the promises of the Zion to come.

Soon we arrived where Ben and Samuel were waiting for us. They asked about my visit to my family and what I had learned from my experience in their world thus far. As I enumerated the amazing truths and lessons I had learned, I realized they were doing this for my benefit, not theirs. By repeating these experiences, I was planting them ever deeper into my mind, that I may remember them once I had returned to mortality.

They explained how, quite often, those who are allowed near-death experiences forget much of what they see and hear. Some of it is blocked purposefully, by God. But other parts are forgotten because of the trauma through which they go in re-entering the body and recovering from injuries.

"There are parts of this experience, Lance," Ben explained,

"which will be purposefully blocked from your memory, as well. There are other parts which are very sacred, which you should not share openly. And then there is much which we are counting on you remembering. So seek to write what you recall in a journal once you are recovered sufficiently. The time will come when you will be prompted to write a book sharing some of these wonderful experiences, in order that others may be strengthened, comforted, and inspired," Ben continued.

He waited for a moment in order that all he was saying would be absorbed and understood. Then he stated, "And for one other purpose shall these things be written and shared. That this message may prick the hearts of many, help awaken them to the awful condition to which your country has declined, remind them of the multitude of prophecies which have been given concerning your day, and open their eyes to the fact that these same prophecies are being fulfilled before their very eyes. It is, indeed, that day and time. Your message is not new, but it must be a serious reminder."

His words penetrated deep within me. He had purposefully spoken these words spirit to spirit, that I may have the added benefit of the increased number of senses involved in their reception. Once again the depth and meaning far surpassed the very words.

"Lance, the group of men are here that would like to speak with you," Samuel informed me. I looked to the right of him and saw a large number of men approaching, dressed in battle fatigues. It was made known to my mind that their dress was not what they usually wore, but that the uniforms would help impress upon my mind the gravity of their message and the depth of their sacrifices.

One of the men came forward and addressed me on behalf of the others. He was a young man of slight build and medium height. There was an intensity in his eyes, though he welcomed me with a warm smile and embrace.

He first shared with me that each of these men had died in the Revolutionary and Civil Wars. They had given their lives for the birth and preservation of our country. Many of these men were young and had not lived long before they fought and died. But they were willing to do so because of the fervor they felt for freedom and liberty.

"That word, Liberty, is a most important gift from God," the soldier explained. "God has given each of us the agency to choose what we want in life. He will not force His will upon us. He allows us the freedom to choose, whether good or bad. Liberty and 'free will' or 'free agency,' as you call it, are one and the same. Indeed, it is one of the greatest gifts we will ever receive from God."

The soldier paused for a second, then continued. "The Declaration of Independence explains that there are God-given inalienable rights granted to man by God. This is truth. And the greatest of these is Liberty, for it is true *Godly* freedom. For this and other freedoms we gave our lives; that you may enjoy the great blessings therein."

He then explained how very few kingdoms of the world have ever experienced such freedoms. Very few have known true liberty. He taught me that God has planned from the beginning to create a paradise on earth, or a Zion, in the last days. This great last Zion would be built in a land of perfect liberty and freedom. It was for this purpose the United States had been created. Many of the founding fathers were moved and inspired by God in their work. No, they were not perfect men, but they were some of the very best God had. They had been held in reserve for this day to lay the foundation on which the Zion of the last days, the Millennial Zion, could be built. The Constitution of this nation had been inspired for this purpose.

The young soldier looked back at his friends and fellow warriors. Then turning back to me, he looked directly into my eyes and said, "We have given our all for the preservation of the United States of America, in order that the Zion of the last days may one day be built upon her soil. We continue to serve God in this effort, working upon the people of this nation to continue to choose sovereignty, peace, and freedom based upon the inalienable rights granted by God. We have, and still are, giving our all. Now what are you doing for this cause?"

I was moved to tears. I was touched deeply and significantly. I knew I would never again take lightly the sacrifices these and other men had made for the freedoms we enjoy. I felt a passion to stand up for our great nation. And I felt a humble gratitude to God for allowing me to live in a land of such peace, freedom, and, most especially, Liberty. We have enjoyed a lifetime of happiness, peace, and material prosperity because of the sacrifices made by so many.

And so I must herald their message and echo the question they posed to me, "Now what are you doing for this cause?" Someday, I believe, we will answer at the very judgement bar of God concerning how we have used these profound blessings.

THE MESSAGE

CHAPTER FIFTEEN

The Blessing

My Grandfather Mark stood at my side as I was told of the sacrifices these soldiers of the Revolutionary and Civil Wars had made. Grandpa, too, had known of sacrifice for freedoms. He had been a soldier in World War I. He had seen many of his buddies lose their lives in that conflict. They had fought with great resolve for the freedoms of our nation. He had tears in his eyes, as well. I knew he understood what these men were saying.

Grandpa hugged me, then smiled at me and said, "Lance, your Dad needs to give you a blessing today and he needs to catch an airplane. Come with me."

He took me by the hand and we began to step into the sky, as if we were flying. Everything went foggy around us, then instantly we were standing in an airport terminal. I watched as my Grandfather went to a computer monitor and put his finger on the screen. He thumbed down the information. Whether he was reading the information or changing it, I do not know. Then he said, "OK, Lance, let's go." He once again took my hand and we began to rise into the air, our vision clouded.

Suddenly we were standing on the floor of the Idaho State Senate. As 'Dad' is a state senator and they were in session, my father was present in this large room. I looked to my right and saw my father sitting in his chair next to his seat-mate. He had his legs crossed and arms folded, a studious look on his face. He was engrossed in a debate that was taking place at that moment on the Senate floor. We watched my father as he fulfilled his role as Senator.

As I beheld my Grandfather observing his son, my father, who was carefully considering the impact a new regulation would have upon the people, I could see the pride in his eyes. I could see the love he had for my Dad. I had not noted the resemblance between them until then, but I was moved with a knowledge of how my Grandfather was so much a part of my Dad, as he was also a part of me. Some of his very characteristics had been carried on in each of us, and he watched with pride as his son worked.

A wonderful thing happened as we followed my father. I watched my Grandfather walk up to my Dad and lean to his ear and say, "Mel, you need to give Lance a blessing today, and you have to catch an airplane in twenty minutes."

I watched as my father suddenly reacted with a start, and looked at his watch.

"Oh, boy!" he exclaimed. "I forgot! I am supposed to be catching an airplane in twenty minutes!" He turned to someone standing there and told them that he had to leave immediately. I looked at a clock on the wall. It was 1:30 p.m.

We followed my father as he gathered his things, headed across the Capitol building, crossed the parking lot to his car, and drove to the Boise Airport. I saw every road he turned on, watched him park in long-term parking, catch a shuttle to the terminal, and witnessed him cross the tarmac to the plane.

Grandpa smiled at me. "Let's go, son. You will be fine now."

We headed back into the Spirit World. Along the way, however, my mind was spinning. What I had witnessed was a most amazing thing. My father had clearly heard my Grandfather's promptings and instantly reacted. He had not known his father was speaking to him, nor even that the inspiration came from God. But it had. Now I wondered how many times I had been inspired by unseen ministering servants of God, sent to assist me? How many times had I thought I suddenly had a most important idea and assumed I was the one with such great intellect? I was sobered by the thought.

The experience was a great example of what Randy had taught me concerning how they serve and assist us. Never again will I doubt the influence of God in, even the smallest of matters in my life. He is listening, and His servants are indeed being sent to help us.

THE MESSAGE

CHAPTER SIXTEEN

The Message

My Grandfather and I returned to the Spirit World and were greeted by several of my family. We talked for several minutes, then a foreboding feeling within me seemed to let me know my visit was nearly finished.

Ben and Samuel arrived. Randy informed me it was time for my return to mortality; this time for good. I felt sad to leave these wonderful family members and friends. And to leave a world as magnificent as this was almost unthinkable. I could hardly stand to lose the peace and love that permeated everything. It was a very difficult moment.

Randy shared some additional important information with me at that point. He explained things which would be expected of me upon my return. He told me that one of the conditions of my return was for me to share a message with others concerning some of the things I had seen and heard. I was to add my witness that God, indeed, lives, that Jesus Christ is the Son of God and our Redeemer, and that there is undoubtedly life after death. I was to share parts of my experience in an effort to give comfort to so many who have lost loved ones through death, and help them understand what a beautiful experience those who die are enjoying.

Then I was given one final piece of the message; one which, is also not new, but is crucial for us to recognize and internalize.

I was warned that our nation stands on the brink of self-destruction. We are in grave danger of causing our own destruction due to a number of issues. Several of these were then enumerated to me:

(1) We have turned away from the morals and values which once made us strong.

(2) We have adopted a belief that all truth is relative and changes with time. I was taught in no uncertain manner that truth is eternal.

(3) It was impressed upon my mind in such a way as I shall never forget that God is the father of us all and loves each of us with a greater love than we can comprehend. We must turn back to Him, not allowing Him to become a stranger in our nation.

(4) We must come to an understanding that *family* is the center of *their* perfect society, and that we must not only retain it as the central unit of our society and safeguard it, but vastly strengthen it. For within those walls lie the answers to most of the problems facing our nation today.

(5) I was once again reminded that the founding fathers were inspired in their efforts and that America is destined to become the home of the New Jerusalem, the Zion of the last days, where all people who desire may reside in peace and love. I was told that God will

protect America and her people as long as we serve Him. I was shown that if we do not turn back, as a people, to God, family, and country, we will soon self-destruct and be destroyed. It was explained that though many would choose this course of self destruction, many others would desire the peace of God, and the freedoms and liberty of a Zion; a society such as theirs.

A great truth was then shown me. "The greatest principle in the creation of a society such as ours is *Service*," Samuel said. "Each person in our society is involved in service to others continually. It is the mode of Heaven. It is one of the great eternal principles that creates a heaven. Each seeks for the betterment of the whole, not themselves. Each seeks to serve God, our Father, through following His command of 'Love One Another,'" Samuel continued.

"Service is the action form of loving one another. When you truly love someone, you seek to serve them. Your concerns are for their happiness and welfare."

Ben then explained to me that if the people of this nation would go out and begin serving—first the members of their families more fully, then their neighbors and community, and then their extended family (their brothers and sisters of their nation)—it would do more to change the hearts of this people than any other thing that could be done.

"If you will go out and serve one another," Ben continued, "you will learn to love one another in a way you have never experienced before. If you will serve one another, you will love God and grow closer to Him. And if you will serve one another, your nation will be transformed into a haven of real peace and freedom. It will, indeed, become a Zion one day."

My mind was filled with the incredible lessons I was learning of truths, principles, and ideals. I thought about what I had just been told. God, family, and country were crucial to our survival. And if we sincerely loved one another we would serve each other. Sure, I knew of Service, but now it was being explained as a major principle of a Paradise, and the most important thing that, as a people, we can do to change our awful state.

As we serve our wives and children, we will love them more, and we will become closer. Our very hearts will be changed. If we will serve our neighbors and communities, we will break down the barriers which divide us and cause a peace and love to permeate our cities. And if we will serve our brothers and sisters of this nation, we can cause a day of Zion, a day of complete peace, to come. Such a day this world has never seen. As I had experienced in their world, this love and peave will become contagious. Without a doubt, we could make it spread. With love and peace such as this, who would ever want to leave?

I knew that this message was for me and my family. But I recognized, also, that it can indeed be a poignant reminder to others of the surety of the prophecies which have been given concerning our day, and the need to strengthen ourselves and our families for that which certainly must be. And, perhaps, also, it can be a reminder of the incredible power of Service, and its ability to transform us as a people.

"Randy, will people understand my purpose in sharing such a message?" I asked, my heart filled with the fear of my inadequacy. I knew my abilities are so limited in trying to share such a story.

"Lance, there will be some who will not. But those who sincerely seek to know whether it is truth will feel it is so by the same witness you have experienced. The Spirit accompanies all truth, and it shall witness with warmth and new light and understanding to those who desire to know."

He smiled and hugged me. "I know it is difficult, but God shall sustain you. It is time. Your world stands on the edge of the millennial era. There is much that will transpire in this day."

I hugged him again and thanked him profusely for all he had done. It was hard to leave him. We had become extremely close through this visit. I embraced each of my family and friends and asked them to continue to pray for us and watch over us.

I would never again question whether God was watching over me. I had come to an absolute knowledge of His love for each of us, and I could never forget it.

It was time. As much as I desired it to last a bit longer, it was finally time I must leave. With a tearful goodbye, I stepped back into mortality.

THE MESSAGE

CHAPTER SEVENTEEN

Return To Mortality

The faint sound of voices filtered into my mind as I began to leave the comatose state. It all seemed so distant. I had been enduring countless nightmares in which I was suffocating and would come ever so close to dying. In each of these dreams I had loved ones around me encouraging me to continue fighting and telling me how much they loved me.

Now as I began to come out of the coma and experience some sense of reality, I was not so sure that these faint voices I was hearing around me weren't some of the very same voices I had heard in my dreams.

I could hear a compassionate voice calling my name and begging me to respond by opening my eyes. The voice became louder and the tone more familiar as I neared a level of partial consciousness. It was the voice of my mother.

"Lance, can you hear me?" Mom questioned. "Lance, we love you, honey. Can you hear any of us?" She turned to the nurse standing in the room. "I still can't see any response. Are you sure he is coming out of the coma right now? Maybe he needs another day before he can reach a real level of responsiveness."

"No," the nurse replied, "I am seeing some major improvement in him. It shouldn't be long now before he's awake. Remember, though, it is common for the patient to feel terrified when they find that they are paralyzed and can't move their legs or arms."

"The ventilator can be *very* frightening for them, as well," the nurse continued. "It's difficult to get used to that thing. It's kind of like trying to breathe through a straw! You want to fight it. So, just remember to talk to him and comfort him. Tell him everything is going to be fine. Help him to realize he must not fight against the ventilator."

Terror *did* begin to fill me as I heard the nurses instructions. *Paralyzed? Why am I paralyzed?* I thought. My mind began to race as I pondered this news. With each additional moment a surge of pain coursed through my veins. It was intense! I wanted to go back to the Spirit World where pain did not exist. That had felt so wonderful! But I knew I was not going back again. No, this time I was here for good.

I attempted to open my eyes and let them know I was hearing their words. The light burned my eyes as I squinted under its glare. I tried to move my mouth to speak, but there was no sound.

"He's moving his mouth," my mother exclaimed. "He's beginning to wake up!"

I tried again to say a word or two, but there was no sound. *Why is there no sound?* I thought. I attempted to move my hand to my mouth but found that I could not.

"Lance, can you hear me, honey? It's me...Mom. You've

been gone for a very long time. You are paralyzed with drugs to help you not exert too much energy. Don't fight it," Mom continued.

I felt a sudden need to take a breath, but again, I could not. I began to panic as I started trying to suck harder and harder. *Something is seriously wrong,* I thought, certain that I should be getting more air.

The nurse understood my reaction and put her hand on my shoulder, trying to calm me. "It's alright, Lance. Don't fight it. You have a machine placed in your trachea called a ventilator. It will breathe for you. Don't you try to force a breath, it will do all the work for you for awhile.

She seemed so tranquil, but I felt anything but peace. *She doesn't understand that this machine isn't working! I am not getting near enough air to survive!* I thought, my eyes now opening wide with fear. *I am suffocating again!*

Both the nurse and my mother were holding my shoulders now, trying to assure me that all was fine, but I could not believe this was what I was supposed to be feeling. I exerted every muscle I could find to raise myself and fight for the air I needed to live, but with the medications yet paralyzing my muscles, it was a weak attempt. The one set of muscles that seemed to function were to my neck, and I tried to thrash in an effort to let them know I was suffocating. I tried again and again to speak, but the tubes which had been inserted into the incision in my neck made it so that no air passed by the vocal chords.

"Lance, settle down. You are fine, you will be just fine.

Don't fight it!" the nurse continued.

I could not believe, however, that she knew what I was experiencing. It was terrifying. I was suffocating all over again.

My mother's eyes were filled with tears now. She could not stand to see me in such pain and confusion. She understood what the nurse had told her, but she clearly could see I could not. "Oh, please help him! He's suffocating! He must not be getting enough air!"

The nurse tried to assure her that this was normal, but it didn't make it any easier. Finally, the nurse inserted a needle into my IV line and began to sedate me. Sleep could not have been more welcome.

"We will bring him up out of the sedation for an ever increasing period of time for the next few days as he becomes aware of his condition and more comfortable with the ventilator," the nurse informed my mother.

Her heart ached for me and the apparent terror I had experienced. She could not hold back the tears, even with the nurse still present. "Thank you for your help. I ....I hope it starts getting easier for him."

"It will. It really will. I know it is difficult to watch, but there is no other way. His body is not able to breathe on its own yet." The nurse placed a hand around my mother's shoulder and gave her a comforting hug.

"The next several days were near replays of the same experience. My mother and my wife tried to be present each time I was awakened, but it was very difficult to bear, for each of us. Jozet had hoped she would have a chance to finally speak to me after several weeks, but instead she saw a face filled with terror and no comprehension of what they were trying to do for me.

Each time I awakened it was a bit easier to discern the faces and words being spoken to me. Each time it became more apparent what I had to do to be able to stay awake. I had to learn not to fight *that machine,* and I had to somehow relinquish to it my power to breathe.

My body had filled with a rare form of staph infection called MRSA. There is only one drug that is usually able to kill it, and so far it had not worked for me. Consequently, anyone coming into the room with me had to wear gloves, gown, and mask. The infection was so contagious that they would not allow my smaller children to come visit me.

After many days I was being kept awake for longer periods of time. I was very anxious to talk, but now understood it was not possible. I would mouth words to my family and nurses, but it was very difficult for anyone to understand what I was trying to say. I sought to communicate in one or two word phrases. Anything longer seemed to be completely lost.

Several times I tried to say, "I have been there," and let my family know that I had been to the Spirit World. I wanted desperately to tell them of the experiences I had, but no one could understand what I was trying to share. I finally gave up, deciding to wait until they took *the machine* out of my throat so I could speak.

My sister, Pam, my brother Mark and his wife, Teresa, came

and sat with me often. They were so kind to help me. Each would rub my aching legs for hours. It gave me relief that was deeply important at that time.

The pain continued to be very intense, and the pain medication seemed to barely lighten it. Each day was an eternity; each night a continuation of the nightmares.

The more I became cognizant of my condition, the more I desired to be able to move again and take care of even the most menial tasks on my own. It was nearly two weeks before I had enough strength in my arm to raise my hand and scratch my nose.

My father and mother were visiting me when I finally accomplished this. The itching had defeated my patience, and I was bound and determined to relieve it on my own. I slowly lifted my skeleton of an arm toward my face. Each inch closer was a new record for me. At long last my finger reached my nose and I scratched. It felt so good to be able to accomplish such a feat.

"Hooray!" my Dad yelled out through his mask. "He touched his nose!" We all laughed to think that such an experience could be considered triumphant, but it was.

Though the recovery seemed ever so slow to me, the doctors were amazed with my daily progress. "I can't tell you how wonderfully you are progressing, Lance," Dr. Krell would tell me. "You really are improving markedly every day. We are very pleased."

I appreciated their encouragement and reports. They, too, had witnessed the miracle which had occurred. None of us could deny it. There was no logical reason for my being alive. I witnessed on more than one occasion my doctors wiping away tears after tenderly hugging my wife and mother. They could not have been more compassionate in their care of me and my family. And the nursing staff were amazing, as well. There were some tough days to endure, emotional moments to abide, and large mountains to scale in my recovery process. They were ever the compassionate professionals as they sought to help me rehabilitate and heal. I came to appreciate and realize how difficult their jobs are in such a case.

One day I asked, in my two word phrases, how long until I would be able to go home.

"Honestly, Lance?" the nurse asked me. I nodded. "For someone with as many problems as you have, it very honestly could be a year." Tears began to fill my eyes. I tried to hide my inner pain, but I couldn't. I wanted to be able to go home to my family. I hadn't seen my younger children for nearly three months now, and I was desperately wanting to see them.

"You want to be home with your family, don't you, Lance," my nurse said looking into my tear filled eyes. I nodded emphatically. "Let me see what I can do for you," he said, and out the room he headed. A few minutes later he returned, replaced the gown, mask, and gloves, and walked to my side.

"Lance, I have received permission for your little daughter and son to come up and see you through the glass. Would you like that?" he asked. My heart melted. I nodded my head and tried to thank him with my eyes. I could not think of another thing until they came the next evening.

My wife held them to the window and told them to say "Hello to Daddy". My daughter grinned with excitement. I could only wave and cry. Jozet tried to explain to McKaye why she could not go in and touch me, but Nathan, our little boy, now only just past a year old, could only bang on the glass and reach for me. His eyes spoke clearly his disappointment that I would not come to him and hold him. He banged over and over again, until he could see Daddy was not going to come to him. I couldn't stand it any longer. I mouthed to the nurse, "Please take him away." It had been wonderful to see him, but so hard to watch his confusion. It gave me strength, though, to continue my fight, and renewed determination to heal faster than anyone would believe was possible. I had resolved to get out of that hospital in record time.

The doctors wanted to help me set realistic expectations, so I would not give-in to discouragement. They said it would take, perhaps, three months to learn to speak again, from six months to a year to learn to walk again, and many months to relearn the normal processes I had come to find so automatic. Legitimately, many people take from many months to years to rehabilitate from such a condition as I was in.

There were many difficult days in my recovery process. I developed a terrible rash and boils all over my body. It itched profusely, and hurt, as well. It was decided that it had come from an allergic reaction to the antibiotics they were using to try to kill the staph infection. Though the rash, boils, itching, and pain were extremely difficult to endure, the staph infection had to be killed. So the nurses and my family would coat my entire body with a creme which was supposed to help stop the pain and itching. Then I would lay for the next hour shivering from the cold of the thick lotion. I was so weak that I was unable to rub, scratch, or move to help relieve the anguish. There were nights when I thought I was going to go mad from the intense itching and pain. The sores covered my body from head to toe. I was raw and bleeding. Nothing seemed to dim the agony for many days.

The doctors and nurses tried desperately to find any kind of ointment or medication that could relieve my misery, but very little seemed to help.

Finally, after what seemed an eternity, my skin condition began to heal. I was so very grateful to God for bringing those days to an end.

The day the nurses finally removed the ventilator and closed the incision in my neck was most memorable. It felt so good to hear my own voice again. It brought an entirely new understanding to me concerning the process of speech. What a miracle! God masterfully crafted our bodies to do such wondrous things. One of the nurses brought me a cell phone and told me to call my wife.

"Hi, Jozet. How are you?" I said. I heard her break into sobs and thank God as she realized it was me speaking to her.

"I can't believe it. I can hardly believe it. Oh, I didn't know if I would ever hear your voice again." And for the first time in many months I heard myself laugh, and cry.

As soon as I was able to speak, I began telling my family about my journey. They shared their feelings of having felt my spirit near them. There was no questioning as they heard my story. Each believed fully and completely. As I shared my experiences there were times when I felt that burning of the Spirit inside me again. It was a most welcomed feeling. They felt it, as well, and knew what I was telling them was truth.

One day as Jozet was visiting me, I tried to share with her the incredible feeling of peace that existed in the Spirit World.

"Oh, Jozet, it was the most powerful, wonderful feeling I have ever felt. I would do anything...anything, to have that peace again." Then I cried. I knew that peace was fading from me.

My Mother and Father visited me, not long after I had started speaking again, and commented how great it was to hear my voice. We laughed and talked together, each still masked so that I would not transmit my terrible infection.

Then my mother said to me, "Lance, your Father gave you a special blessing while you were in your coma and things were at their worst. It probably saved your life."

"You gave me a blessing Dad?" I said.

"Yes, I did," Dad answered. "I was over in Boise..."

With the mention of Boise, my memory of the my experience with Grandpa and my Dad flooded into my mind.

"I was there!" I exclaimed, full of excitement to share what had occurred.

"No, I was over in Boise…," Dad corrected me.

"I know you were, Dad. And I was there with you!"

He looked at me with a strange expression. "What do you mean?"

"Dad, I was there along with your father!"

"Dad's eyes became wider and a look of puzzlement filled his face. "My father? What do you mean?"

I began sharing the story of how Grandpa had taken me by the hand and we had gone to visit my Dad. I stepped through the experience point by point and told him what I had seen him doing. I told Dad where he was sitting and who was sitting next to him, and repeated the things Dad said to him as he left.

Periodically Dad would say, "Yes, that's exactly right! And then what did I do?"

I added the next details, then watched his face as he agreed each point was exactly right. I completed the story by telling him what I saw as we watched him board the plane.

His chin had dropped a bit, and his expression was one of amazement. "You could not have known that had you not been there. That is precisely what took place."

Dad and Mom looked at one another with awe. What I had shared with them was indeed what had occurred, and the only way I could have known it was to have been there.

"You know, it was absolutely miraculous," Dad began to explain. "You cannot do all the things I had to do to get ready, and drive from the Capitol to the airport in twenty minutes.

It can't be done. The drive itself normally takes twenty-five minutes!"

"I know," I said. "But Grandpa was helping you."

Dad then shared with me another miraculous part of the story. Dad had flown home each Friday evening on the 5:20 PM flight. Mom would leave me at the hospital to pick him up at the airport, and they would again drive to the hospital to see how I was doing.

Dad would call and schedule his flights for the next several weeks at one time. When he called to schedule this flight and a few others, he was informed that the only seat available on that particular Friday would be on the 1:50 flight. Every other Friday had openings on the 5:20. Having no other choice, he scheduled himself to fly on the 1:50 flight, but was going to try to set something else up, as he would not be finished with his Senatorial work for the week by the time the flight left.

Unfortunately, Dad forgot about all of this until that very Friday when Grandpa and I visited him. Now I understood perfectly why Grandpa had needed to prompt Dad to leave when he did. Particularly in light of the blessing I received later that day under my father's hand.

"I'll bet you had some help forgetting to change that flight, Dad!" I said.

"You must be right," he agreed.

There was another miracle taking place as far as my mother was concerned. She had been sitting with me in the hospital that particular day. Things with my health were at their worst.

One of my doctors had just called my mother into the hall to inform her that there didn't seem to be anything else they could do for me. They could see they were losing ground. It appeared I was dying, and they were not sure I would survive through the afternoon.

Mom was distraught. My family had begun to fear the worst, and Mom was not sure she could handle such news. At that moment, when things looked bleakest, Dad, who had caught a ride with another legislator from the airport to the hospital, began to walk down the hall toward my mother and the doctor. Mom knew Dad should not be home until after 6:30 that evening. To her it was an absolute miracle to have him arrive there at such an important moment.

She cried as they talked to the doctor. She turned to my father and told him, "You need to give Lance another blessing." Dad responded that he knew that it was what he was supposed to do.

Dad went home and prayed desperately for God to give him inspiration as to what he should do and say. He shared with us that he felt words come into his mind which he was to say in the blessing. He said that this was perhaps the only time in his life he had ever felt God inspire him with specific words to say in a blessing. But for some reason it was important at that time.

Dad came back to the hospital, along with my brother Mark, my wife, and my mother. Mark and Dad placed their hands on my head and Dad, in the name of Jesus Christ, pronounced the words of prayer and blessing which had been given to him. He blessed my specific organs to heal and promised that I would heal extremely fast, much quicker than would normally be possible. From that point onward, I began to heal. Most certainly, the blessing had a significant impact in my healing. I now knew why it was so important that Grandpa and I went to help my father catch that plane and give that blessing.

As we finished sharing our thoughts concerning the experience with one another, the Spirit burned again inside of us. It was that *sure witness* which I had learned testifies of all truth. And, indeed, this was truth. Each of us knew it, and we knew that God knew it, as well.

This entire experience was most remarkable. We all knew that there was no way I could have known these particular details and facts, had I not been present. It became a physical evidence of the truth of my journey to the other side.

Somehow it is not too hard for me to imagine my Grandfather standing next to my Dad to inspire him with the very words that needed to be said to bless me with life again. I do not know it is so, but from what I have witnessed, I can never doubt the possibility of such things again.

I continued to heal at an extraordinary pace. Periodically, a doctor would come into my room to visit me and say, "You shouldn't be alive. Do you know that? The x-rays of your lungs were black! I have never seen someone with such bad films recover."

I would agree and happily thank them for their part in my healing. It was impossible not to recognize the miracle in what had happened. And I felt an interesting bond with each of those who had worked so hard to preserve my life.

Finally the day came when I was declared free of the terrible staph infection that had plagued me for so long. It was the final hurdle I had to overcome to be allowed to leave the hospital and begin recovery at home. It was a feeling of absolute euphoria.

What was more exciting, was that I had gone from nearly dead to a point of being able to leave the hospital in five short weeks! A far cry from the year it had been predicted it could have been. But then Dad had pronounced such an event would occur. That part of the blessing was now fulfilled as had been promised.

As I left the hospital there were many thanks to be given and goodbyes to be said. Nearly every department of the hospital had played a role in my stay, and there were many who stopped by to share their joy for my great day of recovery.

There were still problems to overcome. My legs had quit functioning while I was in the coma, and though I had gained some mobility in them again, my feet were still lifeless and had absolutely no feeling. It would be more than a year before I could raise my foot or move my toes enough to walk on my own. To this day I have not regained feeling in my feet or the front of my legs. But I consider it a small price to pay to be able to walk on my own again.

They set up a hospital bed in our home, and Jozet and the boys learned to care for me. But each day I saw strength and life return where there had been none.

One night I fell from my hospital bed to the floor. Jozet was sleeping in another room. I tried with all my might to pull myself to my knees and stand up, but I couldn't. I yelled for some time before my calling finally woke Jozet up to come to my aid. She felt terrible that she had not heard me sooner. I felt terrible that I was still so weak that I could not even stand on my own. It was a tough reminder of how far I still had to go to feel normal again.

I had the time now to tell my family in detail about my experience. When my hands had become strong enough I began typing my thoughts and memories into my laptop computer. I wanted to preserve the experience before I forgot anything.

Before long I was feeling well enough to go in a wheel chair to my sons, wrestling tournaments. All four of the older boys were involved but they had not had a desire to continue wrestling while I was in my coma. Part of the wrestling season was over, but I told the boys it was time we started living again. They shouted with excitement and began practicing again. Only two months later I sat with pride beside my wife and watched each one of them place in the State finals. I was so choked with tears and emotions, I thought I would never regain my composure. It was a day I may never have seen.

One night I took the opportunity to share with each of my children and my wife the story of how I had visited them in their school rooms and Jozet in her car. We cried. I shared something specific each was doing so they would remember the particular day. They did. We didn't feel a need for further proof of the truth of my visit, but it added to our strength.

After several months, I knew I had recovered enough to begin trying to understand the message I had been given and how I might share its importance with others. Thoughts began to come about what I needed to do, and I had no doubt where the thoughts had come from. I felt direction coming to me and I began making plans.

To a large extent, now, two years since the accident, I am healed of the problems which led to my coma. But Jozet and I have never been able to listen to that song she had been singing when I visited her as an unseen spirit, without a flood of emotions filling us. All I can do is shed a tear and thank *God for spending a little more time on me.* I know that if He hadn't, I would never have had the opportunity to coach my boys in their sports again, would never have felt my daughter's arms around my neck, would never have heard my infant son call me *Daddy,* and would never have felt my wife's tears roll down her cheek as I pulled her into my arms the night I came home from the hospital and promised her, "I'm not leaving you again for a very long while. And even then, I will never leave you alone."

THE MESSAGE

CHAPTER EIGHTEEN

There Is An Answer

There were many great and important lessons I learned on my journey into the Spirit World, but, perhaps the most important of all of these was the message I was given concerning *Service*. I have frequently thought back on the words of Samuel, Ben, and Randy concerning this important principle just before I left to return to mortality. They taught me that *Service* was the answer to reclaiming our society and changing the hearts of us, as a people. How so?

Service, as they explained to me, *is the action form of love.* The command to *"Love One Another"* could have easily been worded, *"If you love one another, then serve one another."*

But the word Service has lost its impact, meaning, and importance. It has become nearly meaningless and trite. After all, everyone knows that Service helps people. Everyone knows that Service is good. It is such an old idea that no one takes it very seriously anymore. But it is a principle of truth which has existed forever.

I was privileged to witness the paradise that existed in the Spirit World, and I was taught that the principle of Service had been one of the most important keys in forming such societies. The biblical City of Enoch is an example of a city that became a

Zion, a city of absolute peace and liberty, where all citizens care deeply about one another and righteousness reigns. It was through Service that the hearts of the people had been turned to one another and a "oneness" created. It required a devotion to God, as well. But Service became the action form of that devotion and love towards God and others. When this occurred, *selfishness* was replaced with *oneness*. In other words, each person became deeply committed to the good of the whole rather than their own self interests.

These truths they taught me were powerful and important. I have often tried to do service for others, and have felt the great feeling associated with such actions. But I did not comprehend the **incredible impact** this principle could actually have upon a community and society until my family and I performed a most interesting experiment.

I had shared these truths with my wife and children and we discussed the need to become more involved in service to others. Then one day an interesting idea came to mind.

What would happen if a family were to go on a vacation with the sole purpose being to travel from place to place doing service? What kind of a reaction would they see? What kind of an effect would it have upon them? And what kind of chain-reaction might they see from their efforts?

I proposed such a vacation to my family. Some of the family members thought I had taken leave of my senses, but were willing to hear me out on the subject. We discussed it over and over. The more we talked about it the more excited I became.

But Brock, our strapping teenager, was not too impressed with some of my ideas. Nor was my wife. They appreciated the concept, but felt many of our efforts would have little or no impact. Each, however, finally decided to give it a try and see what would happen.

We planned a trip for two weeks across six states where we would travel over 2,000 miles. We determined to stop in cities of all types and sizes to see what different kind of reactions to our service we might receive. Some service events were scheduled beforehand, but most were to be spontaneous.

I made a coupon that said, "Sometimes it's just nice to know somebody cares. Have a great day! From_____, and whomever was handing it out would sign their name on the line. At first, this was one of the things my wife and Brock objected most to doing. Neither wanted to give any of these coupons out.

"It won't do any good," Brock said. "People will think it's dumb!"

"Just humor me," I replied. "Just give it a chance. Promise me you will give one coupon out. Then you can quit, if you still don't want to do it."

"OK, but I'm telling you, it won,t work."

"Just try it!" I pled.

We invited one of our best friends and his family to accompany us on the trip. We crossed the state of Idaho into Oregon, caught the corner of Washington, headed west to Portland, then south down the length of California through San Francisco to Los Angeles. Next we headed north to Las Vegas, Nevada, and up through Utah. Finally, we returned home to Idaho.

My family and I have been on many vacations together. But, we have never been on a vacation more fun and rewarding. It changed our lives. It had a most profound impact on each of us. And we learned that often the small acts of kindness mean every bit as much as the big things we do.

Let me just share a few examples of what we experienced. On our second day of the journey we were in Portland, Oregon. Jozet and Brock had already changed their thoughts concerning the coupons. We were finding that these small coupons had a profound impact on the majority of people to whom we gave them. Brock was especially enjoying giving them to the people he saw who appeared to need a bit of a boost.

Being an ever hungry teenager, that afternoon Brock dragged me into a grocery store deli to get something extra for him to eat. As we were making the purchase, Brock turned to me and asked if I had noticed the girl who was helping us. "She looks to me like she could use a coupon." I agreed and told him to go ahead and give her one. After we had paid for our food, he handed her a coupon.

"What's this for?" the surprised worker questioned.

"It's for you. We just wanted you to know we care, and we hope you have a great day," Brock informed her.

The girl looked at the coupon and read its words. Suddenly she broke into tears and raced into the backroom. Brock looked startled. "What did we do?" he said.

"I think it's OK. I think she was touched by it," I consoled him. We picked up our food and went over to a table to sit down.

Minutes later the girl came over to our table. "Here's your coupon back," she said to Brock.

"Why are you giving it back to us?"

"Because I want you to be able to give it to someone else and make their day as you did mine. Thank you," she replied.

"Oh, no! We have lots of them. You keep it," Brock exclaimed.

The girl's face was full of emotion by now. Tears began to appear in her eyes again. "You have no idea how badly I needed to know that someone cared today. I can't tell you how much this meant…" She rushed off again to the backroom in an effort to hide her display of emotions. But this time Brock knew she was alright.

"Wow, Dad. This is cool. I love it!" he said, with a smile from ear to ear.

He had not believed a little coupon such as this could touch someone, but quickly we learned otherwise. Over the next two weeks Brock passed out more of the coupons than any of us. It was not the reaction I would have expected from a teenager, but we came to learn that teenagers, along with many others, really want to help. They just don't know what to do. That lesson became clear one afternoon in Eureka, California.

We had decided to take some large garbage bags to the beach and pick up trash. We planned to do this for a couple of hours, then do some body surfing and swimming. However, we were not able to move more than about twenty feet without someone coming up to us to ask what we were doing.

"Hi," they would say.

"Hi."

"What are you guys doing?"

"Oh, we're picking up garbage here on the beach."

"Oh." They would pause a second, then say, "How come?"

"We just thought it would be nice to do, and it looked like it needed it."

"Uh huh. Where are you from?"

"We're from Idaho."

"Idaho?!" they would respond with a startled tone. "You're from Idaho, and you're here cleaning up our beach? Why?"

"We just wanted to help out." Then we would explain about our trip and the service we were doing. That was always met with an immediate offer of, "Can we help?" Soon there were numerous people helping us up and down the beach. A group of teenagers were having a beach party. When they found out what we were doing, they, too, wanted to be a part of it. People want to serve, regardless of their age. They just don't know what to do.

Even though we had set up service events with homeless shelters, soup kitchens, and others, I wondered if we would be able to find enough other spontaneous opportunities to keep us busy. My worries were unfounded. Service opportunities were all around us. And I came to realize they always are. We become so busy with our own schedules and concerns that we don't notice (sometimes don't *want* to notice) people around us who could use a kind word, a little note, a helping hand, or some muscle to change a tire.

We had taken rakes, shovels, and other tools that we thought we might need. What we should have taken were more car jacks! I had never realized how many people are stranded alongside the road in need of help. We changed more tires, and helped more people with car problems at the side of the road, than any other single activity. One such experience had a profound impact on my understanding of Service.

We were traveling down the highway when someone in the car noticed an elderly woman with her car broken down on the side of the freeway. We pulled over and went back to assess the situation. My friend Bruce and I found that her jack was broken and she was unable to change her flat tire. Bruce went to his vehicle to get another jack. Within a minute or two my boys had exited the car to help us. The smaller children began playing on the hillside near the road.

It took only minutes for us to help the woman change her tire and recover her ambition to continue her journey. We had a wonderful conversation with her as we worked. My wife and Bruce's wife, Janiel, talked with the woman and took turns watching our smaller children on the hill.

As we put the final piece of the jack away and closed the back hatch on her car, my little daughter McKaye came near with a handful of wild flowers she had picked for the lady.

"Here, these are for you," McKaye said with her sweet young voice. Along came Bruce's two daughters with more flowers.

The lady took each of them and bundled them together. Her eyes were now moist, and she dabbed her tears as she bent down and gave a hug to each of the little girls. "Thank you so much. You don't know how much these have touched me," she said.

We said our goodbyes and loaded back into our vehicles. Each of us were filled with happiness for having helped the woman. But as I looked in my rear view mirror to see the woman now sitting in her car, I watched her gently place the flowers in her visor. She bowed her head and began to pray, clearly thanking God for the help she had received. I realized at that moment that she appreciated what we had done to fix her flat tire. But it had been the act of three small girls that had touched her most. They didn't have the ability to change the tire, but they could do something; they could pick flowers to present. Those little petals spoke more love than anything else given or done. I recognized that each of us have a way of touching others, and each has talents that differ. But even the smallest of children have the ability to make a deep impact on others.

We traveled from city to city, state to state, and had amazing wonderful experiences everywhere we went. But there was a very different, powerful, joyous feeling that accompanied us in our vehicles than we normally have. It was a small taste of that same peace I had felt in Paradise. And it changed us forever.

One day, just after we had loaded back in the car after having helped someone, our young son Creed turned to Brock and said,

"Brock, do you know what I like best about you?"

Brock looked startled. "No, what, Creed?" Creed then explained a particular trait. "Thanks, Creed." Silence.

"Jordan," Brock began, "Do you know what I like best about you?"

"What, Brock?" Then Brock shared his feelings for Jordan.

At that point each of our children began telling one another what they appreciated in each other. As Jozet and I listened to the touching statements, she turned to me and said, "There, Lance. There is the miracle of all of this. Sure, we have touched and helped many others. But the real miracle is what this has done *to us*." Oh, what an insightful truth.

When we arrived home, we sat down and recorded our thoughts and feelings and discussed what had occurred. It had been remarkable. I would never forget the day when Jared yelled at me to pull the van over. I did, thinking there was some kind of emergency. But this eight year old boy had noticed an elderly man sitting lonely and alone on a park bench a hundred yards away.

"I've got to go give him a coupon, Dad." He jumped out of the van and ran across the park to the man. As he gave the coupon to the man, there was a look of confusion on the old man's face. Then, after he had read the note, he threw his head back in laughter, patting Jared on the shoulder. Jared looked ten feet tall as he walked back to our van.

We recounted multitudes of experiences we had on our journey. We laughed and we cried together, knowing we would never be the same.

"There's another important lesson I hope each of us have learned from our trip, as well," I said to my family. "You don't have to go 2,000 miles away from home to serve others. You can do it right in your own town, in your own schools, and in your own home. You don't have to go any particular place to serve. The opportunities are all around us." We each then made a goal to begin trying to do one nice thing for someone else every day.

As we came back into the real world of daily schedules and pressing concerns, we had to force ourselves to keep our minds and eyes open to see the needs around us. It is not easy. We realized it can be difficult at times to keep our focus on others. But we came to an absolute realization of the power of Service. In two weeks it had changed our lives, never to be quite the same again. We viewed ourselves and we viewed others differently. We were suddenly looking for the better of the whole, not just for ourselves. It was miraculous.

Two days after our resolution to daily try to help others, Brock came home from school, excited to share a story.

"Dad, I was walking down the hallway of the school and this kid, who is a bit handicapped, was being teased by some other kids. I told them to stop it. "Why?" they said to me. "Because he's my friend," I told them. Again and again they would start to tease him, and I would say, "Stop teasing him." Each time they would ask *why* and I would tell them that he was my friend. Finally, Dad, they said, "OK, Brock. That's cool. We didn't realize he was *your* friend." Then they left. This kid put his hand on my shoulder, Dad, and looked at me with confusion. He asked, "Why did you do that for me, Brock?" Dad, I looked at him and said, "Because *you* are my friend."

I was speechless for a moment. I recognized what that one event could actually mean to an unaccepted boy. To just know he actually had a friend, and that someone really cares. It could change his life.

"Brock, I am really proud of you. You've come to understand how important it is to care about others, haven't you."

"I love trying to help other people now, Dad. There's a feeling that comes that is really…well, I don't know how to describe it. It's cool."

"I know, Brock. I felt it in Paradise. I know what you mean. It can't be explained, you have to feel it."

We hugged one another and I knew the answer my friends in Spirit Paradise had taught me was real. It had transformed us into better people. And it had left us with a desire to share what we had learned with others.

An old sage philosopher once took his pupil to a pond of water. "What say ye. Does the single solitary act of one have a far reaching effect on others?"

The young student thought. "It would certainly affect those nearby, but could not influence those far away, could it master?"

"Watch," the teacher said as he picked up a large stone. He threw the rock into the pond and the two watched as a splash occurred. Waves began to ripple outward until the water lapped upon the shore.

"Not only the rock and the water, but the entire pond have been affected by my action. So it is with each act of your solitary life. Never doubt the far-reaching effect one's act can have on others."

It is truth. Small, singular acts of service can affect multitudes. Each act of service changes a person, then his home and family, his community, and eventually a nation. So, then, what would hundreds of acts of service and kindness do to a community? It would, indeed, transform it. I have watched it occur in my own community.

I was privileged to be a part of a project that was developed to help save the life of a wonderful young woman in our community who needed a pancreas transplant to survive. She did not have insurance. The difficulties from her health conditions had caused a divorce from her husband, as well. She had no children. Her name was Holli. Holli and her family exhausted every avenue possible to find financial assistance for the transplant. There was no help to be found.

Dad, Mark, and I began telling people about Holli and her need on our daily radio show. We brought Holli and her family into our studio and interviewed them on the show, so that people could come to sense of their wonderful attitudes and justified need. People throughout our community were moved. The doctors had stated that she probably would not live without the transplant, and people felt a need to act quickly.

I would need to write an entire book to share all of the touching stories of people giving to help Holli. It was amazing, and it was most infectious. At first, a few of the grade schools began selling suckers to raise money for Holli. Soon, every grade school, junior high, and high school in our area was participating in some way.

I will never forget the day three young brothers came in with a can full of money. It totaled $226. These boys had worked all summer and fall to earn this money so that they could buy a Nintendo package for Christmas.

"Holli needs the money more than we do," one of the boys said to me. "We want her to have it so that she can live." I cried when they left my office.

There were several families who took all the money they were going to spend on their own family,s Christmas and sent it in for Holli. An elderly woman wrote a letter apologizing there wasn't more, but that the $25 enclosed was every penny she presently had.

The newspapers, TV stations, and other radio stations jumped at the chance to help. Thousands of dollars poured in daily. Neighborhoods and civic clubs took up the crusade and put fund raisers together. Everywhere you went Holli was on people's minds. There was a feeling of Christmas like never before, for we were all giving.

Holli became the *carrier* of that contagious feeling until it spread to transform an entire community that Christmas. But it did not stop there. As word spread, we began receiving donations from people throughout the country, as well a few donations from other parts of the world. For a moment, there really was "Peace on Earth, Goodwill Toward all Men," even if it was only in our small segment of the world.

We had a goal to raise $110,000 for the surgery. But when Christmas came, we had raised far more than that. We began telling people to stop sending any more contributions, but still many came into our American Family Institute office pleading to be allowed to just be a small part of the experience and contribute. We were able to use the excess funds to help several other people who were in catastrophic need. It was one of the most enjoyable experiences of my life. And it was proof positive of the ripple effect of service. Without any doubt, it transformed our community.

Each of these experiences are examples of what I have come to learn about the power of Service. I now know that this answer has truth for us, for I have tested it. I have watched it change individuals. I have watched it change families. I have seen it change our community. It works. It *really* works.

And so I come to the close of my story. I know that what I have shared may be difficult for many to believe. Many who read this will belong to different faiths than mine and may have different understandings and convictions. I understand this. But I pray to God that these differences will not cloud the importance of what we can do together, as friends, and as a people. The truths of Love, God, Family, Country, and Service transcend all boundaries and barriers, for they are absolute and eternal.

Often I think back on my experience in the Spirit World and

the warning and message that was given me concerning our people. I was cautioned that our nation stands on the brink of self-destruction, due to the crumbling of our morals and values, our ejection of God from our society, and the destruction of our families.

Indeed we live in troubled times. These things are of grave concern to all of us, for the stakes are exceedingly high. Our families, our society, our nation, and our world are at risk. If we do not join together, as friends and neighbors, taking a stand for these ideals by reinstating them as priorities in our lives, and by beginning to genuinely love one another through Service, we may lose them.

If we will break down the walls between us and join together for our common good—rather than thinking selfishly of our own interests—our homes, cities, and nation may become havens of peace such as I visited in the Spirit World. A *paradise,* a *Zion, cities of consummate peace,* can be created on earth. I know it is so because *they* told me so, and because the holy scriptures are replete with this same message. Because of my experiences, I yearn to see that day and believe completely it is possible.

I am not a guru nor "spiritual guide." I am not more righteous or more deserving than others. I am just an ordinary man who had an extraordinary experience. I bring nothing new to the table. Rather, I am a *Witness* that these things about which I have written actually happened; these things are literally true. I *know* them as sure as I live. The promise I made to share this message is most serious and I hold it to be sacred.

And so I conclude by recounting the words of my friend, Rick, for his words are the catalyst for all we do concerning these matters. "It is true. It is *really* all true."

About the Author

Lance Richardson currently serves as President of the American Family Institute, a non-profit organization dedicated to Rebuilding America through Strengthening the Family. He has been a co-host of the nationally and regionally syndicated radio talk show, "Probing America," as well as creator and producer of the "What's Right With America" radio segment which was heard on over 400 radio stations nationwide. He speaks extensively across the country in seminars and conferences on a variety of topics concerning the family, emergency preparedness, getting involved, and solutions for the pressing problems of our day. He was recently named to the Who's Who of American Business Executives.

Lance is co-author of the books Zion - Seeking the City of Enoch, Zion II - The Long Road to Sanctification, Masquerading As Angels, as well as author of Knotted Gold. He has also produced a tape set called They Saw Our Day in which he relates prophecies and legends of cultures around the world concerning events which are to occur in our day. He has interviewed numerous cultures around the world to obtain these powerful stories.

Lance is a strong Christian and is actively involved in his church. He has served on numerous civic committees which seek to strengthen America,s families and youth. He is founder and chairman of the "Eagles Dare" character building youth program, and the "Holli Fund," a program to financially assist families in catastrophic need. Mr. Richardson has been a coach for various sports teams for many years. He is married to the former Jozet Miller. They have five sons and one daughter. They currently live in Idaho Falls, Idaho.

THE MESSAGE

Do you want to make a difference?

Service programs are coming together all across the country to strengthen our families, communities, and our nation. Youth are forming clubs in schools to do service in their communities, and to help students who are feeling left out find friends and acceptance.

If you have an interest in joining in these service programs, or starting a new one in your area, please contact us at our website LanceRichardson.net or call 1-888-583-9609. We would also like to hear your stories concerning the great experiences people are having through Service. Email them to us at our website at www.LanceRichardson.net

*"He appeared out of Heaven,
nearly 2,000 years ago, and
prophesied of our day..."*

They Saw Our Day
Researched and presented by Lance M. Richardson

Cultures from around the world are telling of the "Great White Brother" who visited their people and the prophecies he foretold of our day. These are their stories.

* Hopi Indians * Kikuyu of Africa *
* Mahayanas of China * Aztecs * Mayans * Tibetans *
* Cherokees * Nez Perce * Pueblo * Iroquois *

Fascinating stories from cultures around the world detailing the prophecies they have received concerning our day.

Only $14.95 for two cassettes

Order at www.LanceRichardson.net

For anyone who has ever suffered and asked the question...
"Why?"

Knotted Gold
By Lance Richardson

Read the story which preceded "The Message!" Knotted Gold is the true story of Lance & Jozet Richardson and how they came to understand that adversity need not destroy a marriage, rather it can bring strength. It is a powerful message about love, overcoming adversity, and building stronger relationships.

Out in paperback only $9.95 each.

Pick it up at your local bookstore or order at our website www.LanceRichardson.net

Nominated as one of the most inspirational books of the year by New York Times Best-Selling author, Mark V. Hansen (Chicken Soup for the Soul)

*What would happen if
two families went on the road
across 2,000 miles and six states
to do nothing but service for others?*

Coming Soon!

Masquerading As Angels
By Lance Richardson and Bruce Miller

The true story about two families spending a two-week vacation on the road doing nothing but service for others! See what amazing kinds of reactions they had from the people they helped, and the incredible life-changing experience it was for them, as families. An adventure you won't want to miss!

Place orders today at www.LanceRichardson.net